Treyton

A ROCKSTAR ROMANCE

J. NATHAN

Edited by Stephanie Elliot
Proofed by Gem's Precise Proofreads
Cover Design by Tiffany at T.E. Black Designs
Cover Photo by Eric McKinney

First Edition February 2020

For my wonderful readers who loved Kozart and patiently awaited this book. I hope I made you proud.

PROLOGUE

Brielle
Age 10

I hurried through the kitchen packed with unfamiliar faces, my straight black dress constricting my legs so I could only shuffle. My mom never would have made me wear something so grown up. But my father wasn't my mom.

"I'm so sorry for your loss, honey," a stranger said as I moved by him.

"Oh, Brielle, we're so sorry about your mom," a woman I didn't know added, piercing a hole in my already broken heart.

"Such a shame to lose a mother so soon," I heard two women say as I quickened my pace.

I made it to the sitting room where a pianist played classical music on my mom's piano. She was the only one who'd ever played that piano. I wanted to tell him to stop. Tell him it was her piano and he couldn't touch it. But instead, tears stung my eyes as I moved toward it, pulled in by the notes drifting from the ebony grand piano. I leaned my bony hip against it, letting the familiar notes of my mom's favorite piece, "Clair de Lune," settle over me.

A tear trailed down my cheek as I pictured my mom during her final days. So pale. So weak. So lifeless. The vision created a deep cavern in my chest causing my tears to fall freely. I wiped my cheeks with the backs of my hands so the prying eyes couldn't give me the same sympathetic looks they'd been giving me since she joined the other angels in heaven—or so Father Murphy said at her funeral.

Funeral.

My mom was really gone.

The room began to close in on me, suffocating me with its sudden unfamiliarity. The voices around me became muffled. A ringing pierced my ears.

I needed to run.

Run far away from everyone and everything.

I turned from the piano in a desperate attempt to run out of the crowded room, but somehow, my hand caught the crystal bowl filled with M&M's my mom kept on top of the piano. The bowl landed with a *clunk* on the small rug beneath the piano while the M&M's scattered all over the hardwood floor. My eyes shot around the spacious room as everyone stopped talking and looked at me. I bent to retrieve my mother's candy, but the hem of my dress tripped up my legs. I launched forward and landed on the floor. The *boom* echoed through the house.

Again, my eyes jumped around, hoping no one had noticed—especially my father. Necks were craned from adjoining rooms and eyes were on me.

Shoot.

I closed my eyes wanting to be anywhere but there. My father would be furious if I embarrassed him in front of the actors and musicians I'd seen him with at award shows on television.

Two arms scooped me up from behind and placed me on my feet. I didn't bother looking at my savior. I mumbled my thanks and moved as quickly to the grand staircase as the stupid dress would allow me to. I shimmied sideways upstairs where I knew no one would be.

With a bowed head, I walked to my room at the end of the hallway, desperate for silence.

"What the fuck do I know about raising a kid?" my father's deep voice carried down the hallway from his home office. It's where he spent all of his time while he was home—twice a month. He usually stayed in a condo in LA while my mother and I remained in our home in the hills. Our normally quiet existence was disrupted by his bellowing voice whenever he graced us with his presence.

"She's all you've got left," his lawyer said as I inched to the slightly open door.

"Can't we hire a nanny or something?" my father asked.

"You *could* do that…"

A nanny? What was he saying?

"Or," his lawyer continued. "You could move back here and raise her."

Laughter burst from my father's mouth.

How could the thought of moving back home and raising me be funny?

"You had me there for a minute, Silas," my father said, taking a sip of his amber colored drink.

The sound of the ice cubes bouncing off the sides of his glass would be engrained in my brain forever because it was the soundtrack to me learning the truth.

The truth my mother was too kind to ever admit.

My father didn't want me.

CHAPTER ONE

Brielle
Age 27

I watched from the side of the stage. Z, aka Kozart Savage the lead singer of Savage Beasts, kneeled at center stage in front of his girlfriend Aubrey. The South African crowd roared, the sound echoing through the outdoor arena like nothing I'd ever heard before. I knew Z loved her, but her time with the band overseas for the summer tour had solidified it. And none of us could deny it. Z was happier when she was around.

On stage, Z gazed up at Aubrey like she was the only girl on the planet.

For him, she was.

I'd been with my boyfriend Keith for a year, and I couldn't recall him ever looking at me with that intensity, with that mix of love and awe, that Z looked at Aubrey with.

And, in that moment, I knew I wanted that.

But did I deserve it?

I'd been wrong to keep Z and Aubrey apart because it *could have* been bad for his reputation as a rock star— the most eligible rock star in the world. As their publicist, it was my job to clean up the bands' messes. It was my job to anticipate future messes. But I had been wrong about their fans' reaction to him being in a committed relationship with a college student. I had been wrong to think an A-list actress would've been better for his reputation—better for publicity.

"Congratulations," I said to Aubrey as she floated offstage, eyeing the ginormous diamond on her finger.

She looked to me all doe-eyed and in love. "Thank you. Did you know?"

I shook my head, just as stunned as everyone else. "Z's good at keeping secrets."

She nodded, that knowing look flashing in her eyes—the look that two people who were truly in love got when they knew something the rest of us didn't. She pulled her phone from her back pocket, likely eager to tell her family the exciting news as she disappeared backstage.

Aubrey had warmed up to me over the past month—us being the only females on tour with the band—but I wondered if Z would ever fully forgive me from trying to keep them apart.

I guess time would tell.

* * *

Glasses had been raised for Z and Aubrey, the newly engaged couple, in the trendy hotel bar. It had been closed off to everyone but the band and crew to celebrate. They were all smiles, stealing glances at each other the whole time before saying their goodbyes and ditching the party so they could be alone.

I watched them leave. A heaviness pressed on my chest, longing to have what they had.

If I was being honest, it's why I'd dropped everything to come on a two-month tour with the band. I never traveled with the band. But I'd convinced myself they needed me this time. I was the only one who could publicize all the charity work and fun they were having overseas.

But that was a complete lie.

I could have hired any number of photographers and journalists who would have been more than willing to travel across the globe with the band. But, the truth was, I needed a break from my life. A break from my boyfriend. A break from my father—my boss. A break from everything.

Treyton slipped into the seat beside me at the bar, his dirty blond hair disheveled and his blue eyes distant. His rock star look was such a contrast to my tight ponytail and thick glasses. He was all bad boy drummer, and I was trendy business suits and attitude. "What's up, Brie?"

"What?"

"You don't answer 'what' when someone asks 'what's up,'" he said.

I rolled my eyes. Treyton and I had a strained relationship. He may have been a hell of a drummer, but he was the band's biggest screwup. I'd saved his ass and covered up the real story more times than I could count.

"Are we ever gonna be okay?" he asked, tossing back his drink.

"We're fine, Trey."

He scoffed, both of us knowing that was a lie.

"Why don't you just go hang with Cam and Marcus? I don't need a babysitter," I said.

He pushed himself to his feet, towering over me with a glare before joining his bandmates at the bar.

I pulled in a deep breath, feeling more alone than I had before he sat down.

I was a bitch.

A complete and utter bitch all the time.

It's what I'd been bred to do. What I watched my father do for my entire life. It's what made him the powerful man he was today. I was just a publicist now, but my end goal had always been to take over his company, Artists Limited, when he retired. How satisfying it would be to run his company and prove to him that I was something. My need to prove to him once and for all that I was worthy of his respect ate away at me. I knew it was pathetic to need to prove myself to someone who had proven countless times that he didn't want to be part of my life. Yet, there I was. Doing everything he asked of me. He'd definitely given me the Savage Beasts job because he didn't believe they'd make it as a band. But they had, and I hadn't failed. And now, five years later, they were the company's biggest client.

And while the guys viewed me as a bitch, I didn't care. I was there for two reasons. I kept them out of trouble in the press and made them a shitload of money.

I finished my drink and slipped out of my seat, making my way out of the bar and down the slightly shifting hallway. The designs in the multi-colored carpet swirled to life as I attempted to put one foot in front of the other.

Dammit.

How much had I drunk?

"Brie."

I grasped hold of the wall and turned slowly.

Trey's lips twitched as he moved toward me, his swagger firmly in place. I assumed that swagger—mixed with his insanely good looks, tongue ring, and tattoos— was what got him so many girls. "You okay?"

"Isn't that usually my line?" I asked, a slight slur to my words.

He scoffed. "You mean before or after you ream me

out for fucking up?"

I cocked my head. "I don't ream."

"Bullshit."

"I forcibly make my thoughts known."

He rolled his eyes as he flicked his tongue ring, the silver ball catching the hallway lights. "Let me walk you to your room."

I lifted my brows.

He laughed. "That wasn't a line. I just wanna be sure you get back safely."

"Words I never thought I'd hear uttered by Treyton Collins."

"I'm not always a dick."

"You mean thinking with your dick?" I asked.

"Wow. You're full of the lines tonight, aren't you, Brie?"

He was the only one I let call me Brie, and normally he didn't do it in front of the others. Truth was, even though he pissed me off ninety-nine percent of the time, I'd spent the most time with him—cleaning up his messes. Which made us...if nothing else...frenemies.

I stopped outside the elevator and pressed the button, nearly tripping over my own feet as I stepped back. *Good one, Brie.*

"How much did you have to drink?" he asked as he stepped beside me.

His woodsy scent, a mix of cedar and pine, floated around me, and I hated that I noticed his freaking scent. "I can ride an elevator just fine on my own."

He didn't bother looking at me. "The spoiled child act doesn't suit you, Brie."

I clenched my teeth, stopping myself from saying something I may regret. The elevator doors split apart, and I stepped inside.

Trey stood there staring at me, probably wondering if I'd knee him in the balls if he followed me inside. "Try loosening that ponytail sometime," he said.

My face scrunched, knowing my ponytail was firmly in place.

"Maybe it'll help you relax and get that stick outta your ass for once in your life."

My breath caught in my throat as the doors closed me inside alone.

As much as I hated to admit it, his words stung. Probably because they confirmed what I already knew he really thought of me. What they *all* really thought of me.

CHAPTER TWO

Treyton

Sweat dripped down my face as I pounded away at the drums. Z's voice echoed through the Australian outdoor stadium as the crowd of fifty thousand sang along. That shit never got old. These fans loved us. Loved every song we released. Loved every move we made. It was nice to be on top of the fucking world.

Z finished the lyrics, and the guys and I wrapped up the instrumental. As the last note drifted through the speakers, a half-second of silence passed then the crowd exploded in a wave of screams and applause.

At the front of the stage, Z spoke to the crowd. I took that opportunity to grab the towel from beside my feet and wipe my face. I glanced to the side of the stage where our manager BJ stood beside our publicist Brielle. BJ was a hell of a guy who'd do anything for us. And Brielle? Let's just say she and I had a tense relationship. If you asked her, she'd say it was all hate. And most days it was.

I'd give her one thing, though. She was a pro at making us look like saints, making us a shitload of money on endorsement deals, and cleaning up after *me*. My latest escapade involved the president's daughter. Though by the time Brielle got done with the story, the world thought I'd helped the first daughter raise money for underprivileged kids.

Yup, Brielle earned her money.

But she was a real bitch.

We all knew her daddy owned Artists Limited. But the bastard gave her nothing, except the job, making her earn every last cent she made. Brielle didn't know we knew that, but BJ had spilled the beans one night during a drunken bender.

Z introduced our next song, and I geared up for my drum solo. Each night I amped it up, showing them I was the best mother-fucking drummer in the world. And, tonight in Australia was no different. I owned those drums. And that crowd.

By the time I hit the end of my solo, sweat covered my bare chest. I ducked down and checked the bass drum to be sure I hadn't put the pedal through it while rocking the hell out of my drum set. I held my sticks high in the air and the crowd roared.

Fuck yeah, they did.

* * *

"What got into you tonight?" BJ asked as I stepped backstage after our encore, grabbing a bottle of water and pouring it over my face. "You couldn't wait for a shower?" he asked, noting the water dripping down the front of my chest.

"It was hot as hell out there."

"Speaking of hot as hell…" BJ said softly, before turning and motioning over a hot little blonde standing there in a Savage Beasts T-shirt and tiny cutoffs.

Hello there.

"Hey, Treyton," she said with a soft Aussie accent as she approached.

"This is Zoe," BJ said before spinning away and making himself scarce.

"Your manager said you wanted to meet me," she said sheepishly.

She was exactly my type and BJ knew it. "How could I not?" I said. "Can I get you a drink, Zoe?"

She nodded.

I ticked my head toward the food and beverage spread. We always had the best of everything when we traveled, and Australia had pulled out all the stops for us. I grabbed a water for me and a beer for her and led her to the leather sofa. I sat and Zoe followed me down, the indentation where I sat pulling her small frame right into my side. I cracked open her beer and handed it to her. I held my water up, touching it to her can. "To new friendships," I said.

She smiled, and that's all it took. I'd be getting laid tonight, and we both knew it.

* * *

"Fuck," I groaned as a right hook connected with the left side of my jaw. I bent at the knees, trying to reel back from the fucking pain emanating from my face. My now-glazed eyes focused on the uneven floorboards, wondering what the hell kind of bar Zoe had brought me to.

There were five massive Aussies and one of me.

I straightened my six-foot-two frame, glaring at the even bigger guy who'd sucker-punched me. "I had no idea she had a man."

His eyes cut to Zoe. She looked scared, ducking behind a group of girls who stood by the bar.

"And obviously she didn't mention I wouldn't be welcome here," I said, taking a small step back toward the exit, having already sent an SOS from my pocket. I bumped into something hard behind me. I glanced over my shoulder at another big dude. What the hell did these Aussies eat?

"Where're you going, mate?" His arm shot out and locked around my neck, pulling me into a tight-ass headlock and cutting off my airflow. "You're not so tough now, are you, rock star?"

I clawed at his arm with both my hands, but the motherfucker was huge. I kicked my legs out trying to gain any kind of momentum to get out of his grip, but all it did was give him a chance to lift me further off the ground. I was no lightweight. But this fucker was massive.

"Let him down," Zoe cried. "He didn't know!"

"You sticking up for him?" her man growled.

"I just…" her voice trailed off.

If I could've spoken—or breathed—I would've begged for my life, but I couldn't. Fog crept into my head, and an unfamiliar lightness filled my body. I wasn't gonna make it. Out of all the hell holes I'd been in, *this* was where I was gonna meet the maker. Talk about fucking irony.

Suddenly, the guy's grip loosened and his arm disappeared from my neck.

I dropped to the floor, dragging big gulps of air into my burning lungs. Everything throbbed. My throat. My face. My ass where I'd landed. The muffled sounds around me filtered back into my subconscious.

A thud landed beside me.

My eyes cut to my right.

The guy who put me in the headlock lay beside me, passed out on his side.

I looked up.

Reggie, our bodyguard, stood above me, looking

ready to hurt any fucker who tried him. He pulled me to my feet and pushed me out the front door, using his body to shield mine. None of the others dared take him on or follow us out of the bar.

Reggie shoved me into the backseat of the waiting car and slammed the door, disappearing back into the bar.

I watched out the window. No one came or went as I massaged my sore neck and flexed my throbbing jaw. I rested my head back on the headrest, realizing how fucked I could've been had Reggie not shown up.

The back door flew open.

Instinctively, I shuffled away from it.

"Relax," Brielle said, sliding in beside me.

"Where'd you come from?"

She tipped her head. "You didn't notice me from your spot on the floor?"

Inwardly, I groaned. Why did Reggie have to bring her? I hated her seeing me looking weak—not to mention the condescension written all over her face. "I could've handled it," I lied.

"Yeah, well, *I* handled it," she said, pulling an ice pack out of her handbag and smacking it to activate it. She held it out to me.

I crossed my arms, refusing to accept it. I knew I looked like a sullen child. But, she always handled it. And I was starting to resent her for it.

"You're welcome," she said, dropping the ice pack on my lap. She retrieved a bag of M&M's from her handbag and tore into them. Anything so she didn't have to talk to me.

I said nothing. It had been a long time since I'd thanked her. Or Reggie for that matter. But we paid them for shit like this. They should've been thanking *me*. If I didn't keep screwing up, they'd have nothing to do.

Silence filled the backseat as our driver, with Reggie now beside him in the passenger seat, drove us back to the hotel.

When the throbbing in my cheek felt like a bass drum pounding in my entire body, I finally picked up the ice pack and held it to my cheek. "Why are you even here?" I asked.

Brie's green eyes, beneath thick-rimmed glasses, cut to mine.

"Overseas," I clarified. "You never travel with us."

"I've been on tour with you for a *month*, and you're just asking me why I'm here *now*?"

"Yeah."

She shook her head, her dark ponytail swinging from side to side. "Are you really that dense?"

My eyes narrowed. "What's that supposed to mean?"

"I can't exactly clean up after you from continents away."

"Screw you, Brie." I looked out my window and didn't say another word. I'd been jumped by a group of massive Aussies and now she was gonna give me shit. No. Fucking. Way.

Once we reached the hotel's back door, Reggie held it open. I jumped out of the car without saying a word to anyone. I made it into the hotel, climbed the stairwell to the third floor, and entered my room. No one—not Reggie or Brielle—was going to make me feel worse than I already did.

Brielle

That son of a bitch.

I'd learned early on that being a publicist could be a

thankless job, but not until I met Treyton, did I truly understand what that meant. Reggie and I saved his ass night after night, and he didn't see fit to acknowledge the effort it took.

Treyton had perfected the art of purposely not thanking us. And it was pissing me the hell off. But I had news for the spoiled drummer boy. I wasn't going to put up with his shit any longer.

I stepped inside my hotel room, pulled off my glasses and tossed them on the dresser, then dropped onto the bed. I shouldn't have felt so exhausted. I was twenty-seven for God's sake.

My phone buzzed in my handbag. I slipped it out to find a text from my boyfriend Keith. **You up?**

I texted him back. **Yup.**

Miss you.

I pulled in a breath, surprised by his words. **Oh yeah?**

And then there were no more bouncing dots. I probably should've reciprocated his sentiment. I probably should've done a lot of things.

Keith hadn't wanted me to go on tour with the band. Two months overseas was a long time. But, the truth was, our relationship was part of the reason I wanted to go. I needed to see if absence made the heart grow fonder. Needed to see if that spark I felt the night we met underneath the LA stars would reignite. Needed to see if I'd actually miss him.

I couldn't blame Keith for being short with me. I was lonely, too. I wanted to sleep next to someone. I wanted someone to hold me. I wanted to have a shoulder to lean on when the job became too stressful—when *Treyton* became too stressful.

But, I was beginning to see, I didn't necessarily need *Keith* for those things.

Maybe the job had just hardened me.

It definitely required me to act less human. My game face was always intact, never faltering. It couldn't. I was in a dog-eat-dog world. And I was a pit bull. I had to be. Publicists were disposable in this business. I needed to keep this job and prove myself to everyone.

I tossed my phone down on the nightstand and didn't even bother getting undressed. I climbed under the sheets and an uneasy sleep pulled me under.

CHAPTER THREE

Brielle

Changing countries like underwear was wearing on me. It was three in the morning in New Zealand, and my eyes were wide open. There was no shot in hell I'd fall back asleep, so I climbed out of the hotel bed and rummaged through my luggage. I knew I had some shorts and a sports bra in there somewhere. I pulled them out and threw them on, shoving my feet into my sneakers as I grabbed my keycard and made my way down the elevator to the lobby. The *deserted* lobby.

No one even stood at the front desk as most guests were not arriving in the middle of the night.

I heard soft piano music as I walked through the lobby. My chest constricted ever so subtly. The sound always brought me back to the days when my mom would play for me. My eyes scanned the large space, stopping on the black grand piano in the corner where the music drifted from.

My head hitched back at the sight of Treyton at the piano.

I stopped in my tracks, leaning against a far wall and watching him play. I'd heard he could play multiple instruments, but in the band, he only ever played drums. I'd never been privy to hearing him play the piano. And he was good. *Damn good.*

Lost in his rendition of some classical piece I didn't recognize, he didn't see me standing there.

I wondered why he was awake at three in the morning. Had jet lag plagued him too, or was he just a restless sleeper? And, out of everything he could've been doing—and usually was, why had he opted to play a concert for a deserted lobby?

"You gonna stand there gawking all night?" his deep voice echoed through the lobby.

Dammit. "I wasn't gawking."

He didn't look at me as he continued playing. "Bullshit."

Even though it was empty, there was no point yelling across the lobby, so I walked over. "I'm just surprised."

"That I can play?" he asked.

"That you're good."

He scoffed, never missing a note. "Ask the ladies how good I am."

"I've never seen one back for seconds," I said.

A crooked smirk tipped one side of his mouth. "You've been keeping track?"

I rolled my eyes, though his eyes hadn't moved from the keys to see my expression. "Why are you down here?"

"I could ask you the same question," he countered, the bruising on his jaw less prominent.

"I asked first."

His playing filled the silence that stretched between us.

Was that his answer? Was he really not going to tell me? Were our interactions always going to be so strained?

"Something's gotta give, Brie," he finally said, breaking the standoff.

"What do you mean?"

"This tension." He finished his song. As the last few notes faded into thin air, his eyes cut to mine. "I wouldn't want to mistake it for sexual tension."

I choked on a laugh. "I have a boyfriend."

He glanced around. "I don't see him here. And now that you mention it, I've known you for what? Five years? And I've never met him."

"I keep my work and personal life separate."

His eyes roamed slowly over my body, and I'm sure he was noticing my sports bra and way-too-short shorts. "Is that so?"

I nodded, crossing my arms to cover my chest. In doing so, I revealed my bare stomach.

"Nice belly button ring."

Dammit. "It was a college mistake."

"They come out," he challenged.

I straightened my spine. But I knew, the upper hand I'd normally held by wearing my armor—my business suit, resting bitch face, glasses, and tight ponytail—was gone. I was a superhero without her cape. And I'd never felt so vulnerable under anyone's gaze. "You haven't answered my question, Trey. Why are you here?"

"And you never answered mine, Brie. Why are *you*?"

I growled, hating that I let him annoy me so much. I was a professional. Why was I bantering with an immature drummer? Realizing neither of us was going to back down, I did the only thing I could. I turned away from him and headed to the gym.

"Nice shorts," he called, clearly watching as I walked away. "Your man know you let other guys see so much of your ass?"

"Careful, Trey. There's this thing called sexual

harassment in the workplace. I wouldn't want to mistake your comment for that."

Treyton

What the hell was that?

My fingers itched. I stretched them out and began to play "Clair de Lune" on the piano. It had been one of the first songs I'd learned when my parents bought me a piano.

I had an ear for music at a young age. Once I heard a song, I could just play it. A savant I was not, but my parents spoiled me with every instrument they could get their hands on, and I just began teaching myself to play without any formal training.

I knew others would've been envious of my punk ass being able to play so well, but I needed the outlet. Being born addicted to heroin had not been the easiest start to life, but I escaped seemingly unscathed thanks to my parents who adopted me. Who knew where I would've ended up if they hadn't.

I glanced up from the keys, not needing to look to play. I scanned the empty lobby thankful that Brie hadn't stuck around. I hated that she'd heard me play. That was *my* thing. I didn't need to share it with anyone.

Most people never ventured to the lobby in the middle of the night, so I normally had free rein if the hotel had a piano. Most modern hotels didn't, but overseas I seemed to find one at every stop. I'd been playing a lot lately. I wasn't sure what it meant. I just knew I needed it. I needed to let off steam somehow.

My eyes focused on the sign that indicated the direction of the gym. Something about those tiny shorts.

That damn sports bra that revealed more of Brie than I'd ever seen before. That belly button ring. They all had me…curious.

Z always said there was more to her than met the eye. He called her a sexy librarian with a stick up her ass. I'm sure he called her more than that when she'd convinced us all that he shouldn't have a girlfriend who was still in college. It made sense at the time. We were so successful with our lead singer being a single guy who could play into women's fantasies. But now I realized no one cared who he dated as long as he was happy.

I'd slowly come back into Z's good graces after that whole ordeal. We still weren't as tight as we'd once been. But I couldn't be sure if it was because I turned my back on him or because he had Aubrey now. He had his new best friend and no longer counted on me for that role.

I wasn't bitter. Growing up and moving on was part of life. But the band ensured we'd always be connected. I don't know where I'd be if we weren't. Z, Cam, Marcus, and BJ were the only family I had since my parents died.

I glanced to the gym sign, wondering what I'd find if I ventured in there. Wondering what other secrets Brie kept from us. But I knew, with much certainty, that nothing good could come from me following her.

Brielle

Tears trailed down my cheeks as I stood with my back pressed to the hallway wall, listening to Trey play my mother's song. His beautiful rendition floated through the room as if an entire symphony played it. And as much as I'd wanted to walk away, I couldn't bring myself to move.

I'd purposely refrained from listening to "Clair de Lune." Purposely eliminated it from any classical playlist for fear of hearing it when I least expected it. The sound of the once beautiful piece did nothing but bring me recollections of a life I no longer possessed.

And as much as I wanted Trey to stop playing the song, something inside me wanted to hear it after all these years. Something inside me wanted to remember the happiness my mom brought to my life. I'd shut those thoughts away for so long because of the pain they caused me. But maybe it was time to remember who I once was. Someone my mother could be proud of.

CHAPTER FOUR

Brielle

A muffled version of Savage Beasts' newest song "Fireflies" filtered backstage where I sat on the sofa texting the office. The audience joined in and sang along to the chorus with Z. The sound of over fifty thousand fans singing along still amazed me night after night. I'd never been a rock fan, but since being around their music, I'd begun to like it. Keith didn't care for the band. He was into rap, so when Trey asked why he'd never met him, that was part of the reason. Telling him Keith thought their music sucked didn't seem like a great idea, so I omitted that fact. I was a great omitter. I learned how to play that game early on. Learned how to walk the thin line between truth and fiction to spin a story.

The New Zealand crowd erupted, and I strained my neck to see what the band had done to get them so riled up. Had Z taken off his shirt? That always got the women going. I couldn't blame them. The guy was jacked. I stood and moved to the spot on the side of the stage beside Aubrey and BJ so I could get a better view. Z's shirt remained on.

Oh. It was time for Trey's drum solo. The women loved that too.

Onstage, Trey could really play. I wondered when his *offstage* antics were going to stop. When he'd steer clear of the trouble that seemed to follow him and outgrow the need to secure a groupie at every stop.

Hearing him play the piano the previous night, lost in his own world, made me wonder what else I didn't know about him. He'd always just been the screwup of the group who I had to bail out of bad situations before they led to bad publicity. But after last night, I found myself wondering *why* Trey was the screwup. What made him seek out girls and trouble like no one I'd ever seen before? I'd never questioned it. I always just accepted it for what it was. Trey being Trey. But now I was…curious.

Before long, the guys stepped offstage. Z disappeared with Aubrey while the rest of the guys grabbed food and drinks and settled in, knowing they'd soon need to jump into the waiting vans to head to the airport.

Groupies filled the area within minutes. I never paid them much attention, but for some reason I watched the ones flocking to Trey. He had no idea how good looking he was. He thought the girls all wanted Z. Girls *did* love a lead singer, especially one as guarded and mysterious as Z. But what Trey didn't realize was *he* was the heartstopper. In the eyes of these girls, he was approachable and fun. I think he thought he was second best to Z. I was certainly not going to be the one to enlighten him.

A little redhead with sleeves of tattoos planted her ass in Trey's lap as he talked to Camden and Marcus. She whispered in his ear, and I watched his face light up and his tongue ring roll over his bottom lip.

That's all it took.

They both stood. He grabbed her hand and they slipped out of the room. It was that easy. *He* was that easy. I just hoped *she* wasn't some big wig's daughter. I wasn't in the mood for cleaning up after him when we had such a long flight awaiting us to Japan.

I ducked out to my waiting car. I wasn't driving with the band to the airport since I tried to give us all space when I could. Once I sat comfortably in the back seat, I texted Keith. **Morning.** I stared down at my phone awaiting his response. With the different time zones, I needed to always check the time in the U.S. to be sure I'd catch him.

Hey.

My thumbs pressed away at my phone. **What r u doing today?**

Work. You?

Flying to Japan.

Oh. That's right.

A sinking feeling settled in the pit of my stomach. **I'll text you when we get there.**

K. And that was it.

The car pulled out of the venue and made its way through the New Zealand back roads en route to the airport. I dropped my phone into my handbag, and my head fell back against the headrest. Our conversations had become forced. I knew it was the sign I'd been waiting for. The one that confirmed that our relationship had run its course. At twenty-seven, I wasn't eager to jump back into the dating scene. There were so many creeps out there. Maybe holding on to a relationship that wasn't working had been a safety net. Or, maybe I didn't want to admit that I'd been part of the reason we failed. Because Brielle Patrick didn't fail.

The car eventually pulled up to a private airplane hangar. I unloaded my luggage from the trunk and made my way over to the private jet. My credentials were checked before I boarded, and I took my normal seat up in the front. The guys always took the back and I tried to stay out of their way. They only partially tolerated me being there. Especially, Z.

I pulled out a bag of M&M's and my tablet. I slipped off my shoes and tucked my legs beneath me. I'd been reading a book and was dying to find out how the unlikely couple would get their happy ending. But I made it no more than a chapter before my eyelids betrayed me.

Somewhere between sleep and dreaming, I heard the engine whir to life and the plane move forward, shaking as it lifted off the ground.

"You're snoring, Brie."

My eyes cracked open and darkness surrounded me. The whirring of the jet filled my ears. I blinked multiple times before focusing on Trey seated beside me. "What are you doing?"

"Sitting next to you."

"Why?"

"I was getting lonely back there."

My nose scrunched. "The redhead didn't scratch that itch?"

Laughter burst out of him. "Scratch that itch? Did you really just say that?"

"Yup."

He cleared his throat before his voice lowered. "You want all the gory details?"

"Not really. Why are you sitting here?"

"I was hoping to finish our conversation from the hotel."

"What conversation?"

He smirked. "You know. Belly button ring. Booty shorts."

My eyes flashed around uncomfortably, but everyone was asleep or wore headphones.

"What's wrong? You don't want anyone hearing…" An evil glint shone in his eyes as his voice grew louder. "You have a belly button ring?"

I elbowed him hard.

He just laughed harder. "What? I'm not lying."

I glared at him, hoping that conveyed my level of annoyance with him.

"I think you're scared people will think we're friends," he said as his laughter subsided.

"We're not friends."

"Yeah, but why is that?"

"I don't know. Maybe because your STD-ridden-self can't keep his dick out of every female he encounters."

"Untrue. Never had an STD because I wear condoms and get checked religiously. *And,* my dick hasn't been in every female because it's never been in *you.*"

I rolled my eyes. "Obviously."

He dragged his teeth over his bottom lip, clicking his tongue ring to the back of his teeth. "Careful, Brie. I love a challenge."

"And I have a boyfriend."

"See, you keep saying that, but I don't think I believe you."

"Why would I lie?"

He shrugged as he reached over and grabbed my bag of M&M's that still sat in my lap. "To keep you off-limits?"

I scoffed. "To who?"

"Anyone." He popped a few M&M's into his mouth.

"I assure you he exists."

"Then tell me about him."

Were we really going to do this? "He's an accountant."

"Sounds boring."

"It's safe."

"Safe's boring."

"Yeah. I should date a rock star."

"It'd be a lot more interesting."

I rolled my eyes.

"How long have you been with him?"

"A year."

Trey searched my left hand, seemingly for an engagement ring.

"We're not engaged."

"Why not?"

I shrugged, knowing the truth but smart enough not to confide in him that we were all but a text away from being over. "We're both busy."

"Sounds like an excuse."

I closed my eyes, the conversation exhausting me for more reasons than one. "Is there a point to all these questions?"

He shrugged. "Just want to know more about you."

"Why?"

"Because it occurred to me that I don't really know you," he said.

For the first time ever, I agreed with Treyton Collins. We didn't know each other. Not at all.

"Let's make an agreement," he continued.

"Oh, this is gonna be good. Please tell me it has something to do with you staying out of trouble for the rest of the tour."

Amusement flashed across his features. "There's no way I can promise that."

"Of course, you can't."

He heaved a sigh. "Fine. I'll try. Take it or leave it?"

"What's the agreement?" I asked, knowing better than to agree to anything without hearing the terms.

His lips slipped into a cocky grin. "I want you to tell me something new about you every day."

My brows inverted. "Why?"

"Because I told you. I don't know much about you and I wanna change that."

I thought for a moment. There had to be more to it. Because knowing Trey, there was always more to it. *But*, if we were being civil to each other and playing nice, the likelihood of him screwing up may decrease. "On one condition."

A slow smile pulled up the left side of his mouth. "What's that?"

"You tell me something about *you* every day."

His smile grew, hitting me deep inside.

He'd never smiled *at* me. Cursed at me? Yes. Glared at me? Absolutely. But smiled? Never.

He held out his hand to shake. "Deal."

"I'm not shaking your hand."

"Why not?"

"Because I don't know where it's been."

His shoulders shook with laughter. "I think you're scared the electricity between us will intensify."

My face scrunched. "Electricity?"

"Don't pretend you don't feel it."

"Oh, I feel something. But it's more like bile rising up the back of my throat."

"And the bitch is back."

I snapped my fingers. "Just like that."

His eyes narrowed and he stared at me for a long time. "She never stays away for long, does she?" he asked, but we both knew it wasn't a question. When the game face faltered, the bitch returned every time. "I'm gonna find out why that is," he assured me as he stood from his seat and handed me back my bag of M&M's. "Oh, and just so you know, I don't sleep with every girl you see me with."

My brows dipped, caught off guard by his revelation.

"What's the good in giving it up that easily? Leaving them wanting more is so much more satisfying." And, without another word, he walked down the aisle toward the back of the plane, leaving me and my preconceived notions alone.

CHAPTER FIVE

Brielle

"I can't understand why you're still fucking there," my father barked through the phone.

I said nothing as I paced the floor of my Japanese hotel room, knowing not to speak when he was fired up.

"I need you back here. We've got a new client who needs help."

My head flinched back. "Who's the client?"

"An up-and-coming rapper. Flow House with a Z."

"Flow Houz?"

"You heard of him?"

"Nope. Why does he need help? What'd he do?"

"Gun charges."

I closed my eyes as my head dropped back, trying to think of a way to spin gun charges. "Where was he carrying the weapon?"

"Irene's emailing you all the information right now."

"I'll get working on it as soon as I get it."

"I'm serious, Brielle. You need to get your ass back here. Savage Beasts is a well-oiled machine at this point. You can handle them from the office."

I wanted to tell him that I needed the break. That working for him had caused me unnecessary anxiety. That Keith and I were missing something in our relationship that I thought I'd figure out continents away. That—

"Brielle," my father growled, interrupting my thoughts. "I'm not asking."

Of course he wasn't. He wasn't the type of man to ever ask for anything. It was his way or the highway. The dead air on the other side of the call confirmed that.

I lowered myself down onto the edge of the bed and heaved a deep breath. He'd been right about one thing. Savage Beasts was a well-oiled machine. But didn't he realize I was part of the reason why they functioned so well? Why their reputation never got tainted in the press?

* * *

"I can't play the violin."

I glanced up from where I sat on a chaise lounge in the hotel lobby in Tokyo. I'd been making calls and working on my press release for Flow Houz while waiting for my car to arrive to take me to the arena.

Trey stood in front of me in his usual concert attire: torn jeans and a sleeveless black T-shirt purposely showing his tatted-up left arm. The shading in his tattoos accentuated each ridge in his bicep. I was slowly learning that the music notes, drumsticks, piano keys, and eagles, all interwoven with dark lightning bolts and symbols, were a true representation of Trey.

"Why are you telling me this?" I asked.

"Our deal."

I'd almost forgotten I'd made a deal with the devil. "Why don't you play the violin?" I asked, not really in the mood to do this with him. I had work to do and a father who was up my ass.

He shrugged. "I never liked the sound of them."

"They're making a comeback, you know?"

He lifted a shoulder. "Drums are my passion now."

"I would've thought piano was. You play like you were born to do it."

His eyes widened. "Holy shit."

"What?"

"I think you just gave me a compliment."

"It definitely wasn't a compliment," I assured him.

"Oh, yes it was."

I rolled my eyes. "Whatever, Trey."

With a smug grin, he crossed his arms across his chest, giving me a better view of his biceps. Playing the drums had undoubtedly made them bigger. "Your turn," he prompted.

My eyes snapped up from his arms to his eyes. "I can't play the violin either."

"Lame."

My head retracted. "Why?"

"You totally copped my fact and it has nothing to do with you."

"*I* can't play the violin," I clarified.

"Yeah, but these facts have to be something that says something about you. Who is Brie Patrick?"

My eyes scanned the lobby, focusing in on the golden Buddha with the small pool of water in front of it filled with shiny coins tourists had tossed in hoping to make their wishes come true. Currently, I *wished* I knew how to answer Trey's question.

Who *was* Brie Patrick if not the bossy publicist who got things done? The last carefree Brie I could remember was in college, having the time of her life with her friends, hooking up with frat guys, and just enjoying life. Those were the last good memories I could recall. Since then it's been work, trying futilely to make my father proud, trying to salvage a failing relationship, and being a bitch so people respected me. God, I was a walking cliché.

"I'll tell you what," Trey said.

My eyes flashed back to him as his words pulled me from the truth.

"I'll count that one for today, but moving forward I want something good. Something you don't tell other people."

"Why?"

He smirked, the only answer I'd get as he backed away from me and crossed the lobby to the bank of elevators.

"Ms. Patrick?" a man called.

I swung around.

A young Asian man in a dark suit greeted me. "I've got your car out front."

I nodded, glancing back to the elevators, but Trey had already disappeared.

I pushed myself to my feet and followed my driver outside to the waiting car. The rainy season in Japan had just ended, so the stickiness in the air clung to my business suit. I slipped into the backseat and pulled out my phone, checking my email as we drove through the bustling streets to the concert venue.

When we arrived, I entered through the back door, flashing my neck lanyard with my credentials at the security guard. I made my way to the backstage area. Food and drinks were plenty and the sofas were set up in a square. That way the band would be together preshow and not separate. It was important to Z to create a family vibe. I often wondered why family was so important to him. And why he never discussed his past or family. But if you were in Z's presence for more than a few minutes, you knew those questions were off-limits, and with him, what you got was what he determined you got.

"How's it look?" BJ asked as he stepped backstage, his eyes assessing the area.

"Everything looks in order." I dropped down onto one of the sofas.

"You look tired. Why don't you head back to the hotel after meet and greets?" BJ suggested. "I've got it covered."

I scoffed.

"I'm serious. You're not used to this life. It seems like it's taking a toll."

"In other words, I look like shit?" I said.

His hands shot up. "I never said that."

"You didn't have to."

He huffed, and the way he avoided my eyes as he did it told me I was missing something.

"Spill it," I said. "Did someone say something about me being here?"

He stared across the space between us, saying nothing.

"Who was it? Z? Aubrey?"

He shook his head.

My eyes splayed. "Treyton?"

He shook his head again. "None of them. Though, they're all pretty surprised you lasted this long."

"What's that supposed to mean?"

"You're used to ordering them around from your cushy office in LA. The road isn't for everyone."

"And?"

"And, we may have made some wagers on how long you'd stay."

My mouth opened. "Sons of bitches."

He snickered.

"And?"

"And, Treyton's the last man standing."

My brows inverted. "Which means?"

"Which means he said a month and a half. That gives you two more weeks."

My heart began to thump hard in my chest. Was that why he was being nice to me? Was that why he was trying to strike up a friendship? To get me to stay longer so he could win some bet? "What's he get if he wins?"

BJ shook his head, his lips remaining zipped.

"You told me this much. Why not tell me everything?"

He shook his head.

"How long did *you* think I'd last?"

He tucked his lips, hiding a smile.

"Tell me."

"A week."

"A week?"

He shrugged. "Like I said. The road isn't for everyone."

I scoffed, more pissed than annoyed. I hated knowing I was part of something I knew nothing about. I hated that I was the butt of everyone's joke. I hated that Trey had played me.

* * *

The show ended and the guys made their way backstage. I was pissed at every last one of them for betting on my ability to be on the road. Aubrey greeted Z and they took off, likely back to the hotel. Camden, Marcus, and Trey grabbed drinks and sat on the sofas. I watched them laugh. The sound ate away at my sanity. Were they laughing at me? Were they laughing every time they saw me, surprised I was still there?

Movement near the door caught my attention. BJ ushered female fans backstage wearing tight Savage Beasts T-shirts. Their faces lit up once they spotted the guys on the sofas. The guys, looking equally excited, scooted over and made room for the girls to sit beside them or on the arms of the sofas. I wondered if they'd be able to communicate with the fans without an interpreter. Internally, I held up my hands. Not my problem.

I had a whole new view of groupies now. I'd always believed Trey was sleeping with every last one of them. Now I knew he wasn't, and I couldn't quite wrap my head around the notion since it's what I believed to be the case for five years. Even still, I wasn't hanging around to see if tonight was the night he did.

I turned away and walked outside to my waiting car. If trouble occurred later, the traitors had Reggie to take care of them.

CHAPTER SIX

Brielle

The following morning, I grabbed coffee and a muffin from the continental breakfast spread in the hotel and made my way toward the elevators to head back to my room. Out of the corner of my eye, I spotted Z and Aubrey walking toward the entrance wearing backpacks, their smiles fixed on one another. Camden and Marcus followed a few feet behind. And BJ behind them. Once BJ spotted me, fear swept across his features.

"Hey," I said, my eyes questioning what was going on. I was the one in charge of scheduling appearances so I could control PR that came from those appearances, and they definitely didn't have one.

BJ begrudgingly walked toward me. "Hey."

"Did we have something today I didn't know about?"

He shook his head, clearly trying to avoid eye contact like he had the previous night. "Z just…well, he had an idea for uhhh…for like a team bonding thing."

I cocked my head, obviously not understanding since I was part of the team.

"It's nothing you'd be into anyway," BJ quickly added.

My grip on my plate and coffee tightened. "In other words, I wasn't invited."

"No, it's just—"

"It's fine. I knew Z wasn't going to get over what I did. I just thought
I was slowly becoming part of the team again." I felt myself starting to get upset, but I straightened my spine and donned my bored face. "Whatever."

"Brielle. You wouldn't be into rafting anyway. Your glasses would get wet."

I scoffed, knowing they weren't even prescription glasses. "Have fun." I walked around him and stopped at the elevators. With my plate in my hand, I jammed my finger into the button more pissed than I realized.

The elevator pinged and the doors split apart. Trey stood inside, wearing a backpack. "'Sup, Brie?"

The sight of him so nonchalant twisted a knot in my stomach. Was he really going to act like
it was fine to exclude me? Better yet, was he really going to pretend he hadn't bet on me leaving in two more weeks?

"Sup, Brie?" I asked. "Really?"

He stepped out of the elevator but held his hand there to stop the doors from closing. "What's that supposed to mean?"

I shook my head. "Nothing. Have fun rafting."

Realization crossed his face. "You're pissed."

"Why would I be pissed?"

"Because you weren't invited."

"Nope." I stepped around him and into the elevator, catching a gust of his woodsy cedar scent as I pushed the button for the fifth floor with vigor.

"You are pissed." Trey twisted around and stood in the doorway so the elevator doors couldn't close. "Come with us."

"Oh, you'd just love that, wouldn't you?"

His brows inverted. "What's that mean?"

I shook my head. "Nothing."

"I'm not gonna beg, Brie. Either you get over being left out and come with us or you don't." He shrugged as if it really didn't matter to him. "Your choice."

"I'm staying here."

"Have it your way." He stepped back and the doors closed, leaving me alone inside the elevator.

Being alone was becoming the norm for me. But if I really wanted to stay at the hotel instead of taking Trey up on the offer to go rafting, why did I feel worse than I had before?

CHAPTER SEVEN

Treyton

I made my way toward the rear entrance of the hotel to the waiting van. I was pretty exhausted after rafting earlier, but the show must go on.

"Looks like you didn't drown," Brielle's voice carried through the lobby.

I stifled a grin as I stopped, twisting around to face her. My eyes widened when I caught sight of her hair hanging in dark waves down to her boobs. *What the ever-living fuck?* "Do I know you?"

She cocked her head, shooting me the cut the shit eyes she gave me when I screwed up.

"Lose your hairband?" I asked, motioning toward her hair.

"I had a headache. Sometimes the tight ponytail hurts."

I stared across the space between us. How was it I'd never seen her with her hair down? I thought the ponytail was a permanent appendage. But now...I never wanted to see the damn thing again. My dick twitched. Brie was not bad to look at. Not bad at all. And admitting that to myself pissed me the hell off.

She dragged in a deep breath. "I guess there's always bungee-jumping."

"Come again?"

"Aren't you bungee-jumping in Italy with Camden? The bungee cord could always break."

I laughed. "Did you really just say that?"

"I did."

"That's twisted, even for you."

She shrugged, not even insulted by my insult. "See you at the venue." She brushed by me toward the front door.

I twisted around. "Wait."

She stopped, turning to look at me.

"I don't like heights."

Her brows scrunched, confusion flittering across her face. "So, you're not going bungee jumping?"

"I said I don't like them. Not that I wouldn't do it."

"Why are you telling me this?"

"I owed you a fact. Your turn."

She pulled in a silent breath.

It was becoming amusing to watch her hold back her annoyance with me. Scratch that. At having to be civil toward me.

"I like heights. The higher the better."

"Seriously?"

She nodded, though her tough façade made it impossible to discern if she was telling the truth or not.

"Does that mean you've been skydiving?"

"I'll save that fact for another day…that's if I'm still here."

My head shot back. "You planning on leaving?"

She shrugged, though her eyes stayed locked on mine. "The road isn't for everyone. I'll have to see if I can make it…oh I don't know…another two weeks." She broke eye contact, stepping around me and walking to the door.

I stood watching the door after she'd stepped through it, wondering who'd let her in on our bet.

A tinge of regret formed in my gut for betting on her ability to make it on tour. Or, was it the thought of her leaving? I was just beginning to crack the surface of Brie's tough exterior. There was more to her than met the eye. And I didn't mean someone who wore booty shorts and had a belly button ring. I meant someone with a vulnerable side. Someone whose feelings got hurt when she was left out.

"Hey," Z called from behind me, pulling me from my thoughts.

I turned as he strode toward me, alone for a change. He was unrecognizable to lobby guests with his hat pulled down low.

He glanced to the door where Reggie stood ensuring no fans entered the hotel. As much as he loved our fans, he loved his privacy more. "What are you doing?" he asked me.

"I was just talking to Brielle. Have you seen her today?"

His face scrunched. "Why would I see her?"

I shrugged. "She's just been acting weird lately."

"Weird or bitchier than normal?"

"She just said something about leaving. And her hair was down."

"Down? Like no librarian ponytail?"

I nodded.

"That is weird."

"I'll deny it if you ever repeat this," I said. "But she looked…hot."

Laughter burst out of him. Z rarely laughed unless it was with Aubrey. But he didn't stop. His head fell back and he howled.

"Dude? Do I need to hurt you right now?" I asked.

His laughter subsided. "Do I need to remind you how much she hates you?"

"I just said she looked different."

"*Hot.* You said she looked *hot,*" he corrected me.

Aubrey stepped up beside us. "Who looked hot?"

"No one," I answered.

Z chuckled.

She looked to Z. "Tell me."

My eyes cut to Z's, shooting daggers.

Z shook his head, amused. "Nothing worth repeating." He draped his arm over Aubrey's shoulders and walked her toward the back door.

I scrubbed my hands over my face, needing to snap out of the Brie induced daze I'd temporarily been caught up in.

Brielle

Backstage at the indoor venue, I met with the representative from Make a Dream Come True. She introduced me to Mihoko, a fan who made a wish to meet the band. Mihoko was one of many kids whose dream it was to meet Savage Beasts through the remarkable charity that granted sick children a dream come true.

When it came to charity work, the guys were very generous with both their time and money. And, they'd been granting "dreams" all around the globe this summer.

Footsteps behind the closed door had me glancing over my shoulder. I loved this part. The door swung open and Z stepped through it first. Mihoko, in her Z T-shirt, clapped her hands over her mouth and bounced on her heels. A huge smile spread across Z's face as he greeted Mihoko, wrapping the teen in his arms.

"Why does Z get all the attention?" Trey called out as he stepped into the room, immediately beelining it to them.

Z released Mihoko, and Trey swept her up in his arms, making sure to hold her gingerly as he knew she suffered from an illness.

"I'm tired of the lead singer getting all the attention," Trey teased. "Drummers need love, too."

Mihoko giggled as he placed her onto her feet.

Cam and Marcus received their own hugs before the five of them moved to the sofa, two guys on either side of Mihoko, all giving her their undivided attention. They spent time chatting, laughing, and teasing her *and* each other. Mihoko's smile couldn't have stretched any wider. Mihoko's dad, BJ, Aubrey, and I stood back, giving them privacy while taking in the sweet scene.

Eventually, I grabbed a bag full of merchandise and walked over, placing it by Trey's feet. He grabbed my wrist and pulled me down so he could say something to me. Heat coursed up my arm. *What the hell?*

"Grab me my drumsticks," he whispered.

I blinked hard, trying to ignore the feel of his hand on my arm. "Don't you need them tonight?"

He shrugged as he released me. "I want her to have them. I have others."

I hurried off to retrieve Trey's drumsticks while trying desperately to shake off whatever the hell just happened to me back there.

* * *

The following morning before we left Japan, the band sat on stools in front of a room full of reporters for a broadcast on a popular Japanese music television station. I sat to the side of them acting as the moderator as the Japanese press asked questions while an interpreter interpreted the questions to the band. "What's been your favorite thing about being in Japan?"

"The fans," Z answered. "Their energy is magnetic."

The interpreter interpreted his words, and the reporters applauded, obviously fans loving his response.

I pointed to a reporter in the front row. "You."

She asked her question, and the interpreter interpreted it to the guys. "What's your second favorite thing?"

"The food," Trey said, to the amusement of the reporters and everyone else in the room. Apparently, *food* was a universal word.

I pointed to another reporter. "Next question."

She asked her question, and the interpreter said, "Now that Z is an engaged man, will the rest of you be following suit?"

The guys all laughed.

"That's a no," I answered for them.

"We're just having fun while waiting for the right women to come along," Trey clarified.

Once the interpreter interpreted his response, the female reporters giggled. Of course they did. He was great at the one-liners.

CHAPTER EIGHT

Brielle

The whirring of the plane's engine filled my ears as I tried futilely to sleep. Would Hungary, our next stop, be it for me? Would I relent to my father's wishes and fly back to LA?

"I was adopted," Trey's voice carried into my subconscious.

I turned to my left and opened my eyes.

Trey's blue gaze was locked on mine from the normally *empty* seat beside me. "I hadn't told you anything today with all the press stuff this morning, and I'm a man of my word."

"It would've been fine if you skipped a day," I assured him, trying to forget the feeling of his hand on my arm. My body's reaction had been totally unexpected and traitorous.

"Then I would've missed out on your fact," he said.

The trouble with Trey was you never knew when he was being sincere. He'd gotten so good at the lines that the real Trey was a mystery. *And*, he was only trying to get to know me for selfish reasons. But how could I let him tell me something so personal and not respond? "Why were you adopted?"

He shook his head.

"You brought it up. You can't just squash it."

"I can do whatever I want. The rule was one fact. No elaboration required."

I rolled my eyes, questioning why I'd ever agreed to this game with him. "My father wants me to come back to LA."

He tipped his head. "Why?"

"No elaboration required."

He chuckled. "Fine. You tell me why he wants you back in LA, and I'll tell you the reason I was adopted."

I nodded, surprised he'd tell me seeing as though he'd kept that information under lock and key. "Deal."

"My birth mother was a heroin addict."

My eyes widened.

"Which she graciously passed on to her newborn."

Dammit. The no-drug policy all the crew had to sign now made sense. I'd wondered why that clause was so important to a rock band.

"And, to top it all off, she didn't even want me."

If something was ever going to change my mind about Treyton Collins, this might just do it. Not only was I stunned by the information, but the irony of being unwanted held an uncanny similarity to my life.

"The woman who rocked babies in the nursery took a liking to me," he continued. "She said it was the way I looked at her. Apparently, newborns, especially drug-addicted newborns, don't make eye contact. She said I did."

Goosebumps coasted up my arms.

"She thought it was a sign telling her we were meant to be in each other's lives," he explained, wringing his hands uncomfortably in front of him like he'd never been this open with anyone before. "She said she would've moved heaven and earth to have me."

Tears stung my eyes, picturing this woman willing to fight to have Trey in her life when my own father didn't do the same for me. "She sounds amazing."

He nodded and his eyes drifted away.

I wondered if he too was holding back tears. I knew all too well that it was one thing to possess difficult memories. It was another to tell someone else about those memories.

"Most people don't adopt drug-addicted babies because of the long-term effects." He looked back at me. "It's really an epidemic. Drug addicted babies not getting adopted. They're needy and normally the care is a lifelong commitment. Luckily, for my parents, I didn't have any physical or mental birth defects."

His story was heartbreakingly beautiful. How had I not known any of this? I grasped hold of his arm, suddenly having this need to comfort him. "Trey. I don't know what to say."

He looked at my hand on his arm, and, for a split second, I wondered if my body's reaction to his hand on my arm had elicited the same feelings in him. "There's nothing to say. Shit happens."

Shit happens? Bullshit. He could play it off like it was no big thing, but it's what shaped him into the man he was today. He could play tough, but I was starting to see the truth of what lay beneath the surface.

I removed my hand from his arm, and we sat in silence for a long time. I wondered why he'd told me such personal information. Was it all a ploy to get me to stay longer so he could win the bet? Or did he really just feel comfortable talking to me? I wish the small knot in my stomach wasn't an indication that I liked that idea more than I should. "Tell me about your parents," I said.

Trey chewed on his bottom lip as he contemplated my request. He owed me nothing when it came to his personal life. But for some reason, I hoped he'd tell me more so I'd understand him better. Understand why he found himself in inconvenient situations all the time.

"They were in their late fifties when they adopted me," he said. "That's kind of unheard of because they have age restrictions for adoptions. But child services is that desperate for adoptive parents for drug-addicted babies. I guess they figured some time in a stable environment was better than an orphanage or bouncing around foster care. And I did get a stable environment. For ten years."

My brows dipped.

"My mom died of cancer when I was ten."

I sucked in a sharp breath. Cancer? Ten-years-old? Had the universe been toying with both of us? Was it *currently* toying with us? I sobered my features so the irony rushing through me—and the sympathy I felt for him—wasn't written all over my face. "I'm sorry."

He avoided my gaze, clicking his tongue ring as he spoke. Was that an indication that it was uncomfortable for him to be talking about this? "My dad suffered a heart attack two months later. Some said he died of a broken heart."

Words escaped me. How did I not know any of this? How had I not realized the pain he'd endured so young? How had I not realized the number of similarities we shared?

"I completely understood my dad's grief," he said. "I had double the grief losing both of them in a matter of months."

The knot in my stomach tightened as a vision of Trey, alone at ten, plagued my thoughts.

"They gave me an amazing childhood, but they had no relatives to take me in after they were gone."

I knew what that meant and my heart clenched.

"I bounced around foster care for a while. It's where I met Z."

"I didn't know that."

He stared down at his lap. "I was angry and lonely, and once I became a teenager with raging hormones, it was a lethal combination. Luckily, I met Z when we were seventeen. We had music in common and used it as an outlet."

"Well, I'd say you turned out pretty well."

He choked on his laughter. "Yeah, right. You think I'm a screwup."

"Not a screwup."

"Bullshit."

"It just answers a lot of questions about why you do…whatever the hell you want to do."

He chuckled. "Okay. Enough about me. Your turn."

I sat silently, trying to digest all he'd unloaded on me and wondering how I'd never realized how our situations were so similar. Abandonment, purposely or unavoidably, did a number on your psyche. I could write a book on that for sure.

Trey had backed me into a corner by divulging so much. He'd forced my hand to respond. Damn him. "I'm needed back in LA because I'm representing some new rapper." That wasn't a lie. Just not what I should've told him in that moment.

"And?" he probed.

"And he's needy."

"Needier than me?"

"Time will tell."

He smirked. "So, are you going back?"

I shrugged.

His brows shot up. "Disobeying Daddy? Sounds like a recipe for disaster."

"So, you're saying I *should* go back?"

"You should do what's best for you. Don't you wanna see your accountant man?"

I shrugged.

He tipped his head to the side, his eyes narrowing. "You two break up?"

I shook my head.

"But absence hasn't made the heart grow fonder?"

Admitting the truth seemed only fair after what Trey had told me, so I shook my head.

"Yeah. Life on the road is tough. But it's honest. It hides nothing. If there's a problem in your relationship, it'll amplify it." He stood from his seat and stared down at me.

He was leaving? After everything he'd told me, he was going back to his seat?

"For what it's worth, Brie, I like your hair down." He turned and walked to the rear of the plane, leaving me with not only a compliment but so much new information he'd just entrusted me with.

I'd be lying if I said I wasn't thrown off by everything I'd learned about him recently. First, I find out he doesn't sleep with all the groupies I thought he did, and now this? Who was Treyton Collins if not a manwhore with no regard for anyone but himself? I guess I didn't really know.

What I did know was what it felt like to be unwanted by someone who was supposed to love and care for you. I don't think Trey realized how lucky he was. His birth mother was out of his life once he was adopted. My father still existed. Seeing him once a month after my mother passed away—and him taking calls from clients the entire time and allowing a nanny to raise me, repeatedly reminded me that he didn't want me.

But one day I'd be running his company. And I'd be *nothing* like him. I'd be a hell of a boss. I'd be present for my family. I'd be a loving and caring wife to my husband, and I'd be a damn good mother to my children who I'd lavish with attention.

Falling back asleep after Trey's revelations was a futile endeavor. I sat for a long time with nothing but my thoughts. And what I came to realize was Trey and my similarities were beginning to outweigh our differences.

CHAPTER NINE

Brielle

We arrived in Hungary at three in the morning on the eve of the four-day music festival the band was performing at. Everything had been dark and quiet when the three tour buses we'd be using for the next leg of the tour pulled into the vast artists' parking lot. Now, the following morning, in broad daylight, the buzz in the backstage parking lot was off the charts. Tour buses stretched for what seemed like miles. Canopies and tents provided shade at the sides of the buses and filled the entire parking lot. The smoke of grilling meats filled the air as performers, their families, friends, and roadies mingled while bands played on the main concert stage for over one hundred thousand concertgoers.

Out the bus window BJ and I were sharing, I'd seen the guys, Aubrey, and Reggie take off earlier to mingle with other bands.

I took my time, showering and getting ready on the bus. I dried my hair, wondering if I should leave it down. Trey's compliment, combined with his honesty about his past, sent me right off balance. And as much as I liked being complimented, I didn't want to lose my edge. Lose the respect I earned by dressing the part.

I reached for my glasses from the sink and brought them to my eyes, pausing before putting them on. This weekend was about having fun. The band wasn't performing until the following night, so I wasn't on duty the entire time. I could mingle and meet possible clients.

I lowered my glasses to the sink and stepped back, assessing myself in the floor-length mirror. My torn skinny jeans and black Savage Beasts T-shirt was quite reserved for what most wore at this type of event. And from what I could see out the window, skin was in.

I slipped on some flats and headed off the bus. A soft August breeze greeted me as I joined BJ who sat in a chair under our bus's awning.

"Wow. Look at you," he said. "I almost didn't recognize you."

I sat in the seat beside him. "It's my day off."

He laughed. "You never take a day off."

He was right. I pulled out my phone and checked my email as well as the popular media sources. Flow Houz's gun charges had been dropped due to a mistake made by the police officers who arrested him. So not only did he have one hell of a publicist, he also had a killer legal team.

Once he'd been freed of charges, I released a press release citing a robbery and hold up Flow found himself in as a teenager as the reason for him carrying a weapon. In the end, Flow came out looking like the victim who was just trying to protect himself from enduring a crime like the one he suffered as a teen. Could you blame him?

Flow and I had spoken via video call to flush out all the details, and we'd arranged to meet in person this weekend. Some of his friends were performing and planned to bring him on stage to do a quick rap that I'd been told would bring down the house—pun definitely not intended. The PR from that cameo would be amazing for his budding career. And since we arranged to meet, my father couldn't force me to come home yet.

"Look who came out of the library," Z said.

I glanced up from my phone.

Z and Aubrey stood in front of me. Z wore his signature smirk. And Aubrey of course looked spot-on in her cowboy boots, cutoffs, Savage Beasts tank top, and massive engagement ring showing everyone she was taken.

"Yup. They gave me a day off." I gave Z my own smirk.

Aubrey assessed my casual clothes. "You look good."

"Thanks." I tried not to sound as grateful as I felt. Apparently, I was starved for attention.

Aubrey glanced to Z. "Go back and find the guys. Brielle and I are gonna go score ourselves some drinks."

Z's eyes nearly burst from their sockets. One, because she was telling him to get lost. And two, she wanted to hang out with *me*—the one who tried to break them up because their relationship would be bad for publicity.

I didn't blame him. I was just as stunned as him. Maybe she needed some female companionship too.

"Fine," he said with skeptical eyes. "But keep your phone handy just in case I need to find you."

She planted a kiss on his lips. "Don't let any groupies touch your ass."

His head dropped back and he laughed, the raspy sound bringing a huge smile to her face. "I won't if you won't."

She laughed.

"I'll find you in a bit," he said, before turning and searching the crowded area for Trey, Camden, and Marcus.

"I hope you like Jell-O shots because Lucid Dreams is serving them," Aubrey said as we made our way into the crowd.

"Jell-O shots? I haven't had those since college."

"Yeah, well, I'm still technically *in* college, so…" Aubrey shrugged.

Shit. "I'm not knocking them," I backpedaled, trying to fix what I'd said. "I love them. They bring back good memories."

She smiled. "Relax. I knew what you meant."

It would've been just my luck to ruin the day before it even started.

We walked through the crowd, making our way over to a group of tour buses with skull logos on the sides.

"Oi, ladies," a guy with a mohawk called with a full-blown British accent.

Aubrey glanced to me, amused.

"Hey," I said, greeting him at the tiki bar he and his band had set up.

"I'm Noah." He eyed me up and down. "And who might you be, love?"

"Brielle. And this Aubrey."

"Pleasure," he said. "So, what'll it be, loves?"

"What are you serving?" Aubrey asked.

"Only the finest Jell-O shots on this side of the pond," he assured us, holding out two small plastic cups with red Jell-O inside. We reached for the shots, but he pulled them back. "Not until you tell me your favorite band."

I glanced down at my Savage Beasts T-shirt.

His head fell back. "Seriously?" He glanced to Aubrey. "I knew you looked familiar. You're Z's girl."

"Guilty," she said.

Noah's eyes cut to mine. "Then who are you, love? Treyton's girl?"

Laughter burst out of Aubrey. "Brielle and Treyton? Yeah right."

I laughed too. Treyton and anyone other than a one-night stand was comical.

Noah handed us the Jell-O shots, and the three of us tipped back our heads and swallowed them.

"Mmmm," I said, not meaning to say it aloud, but the slimy texture brought me right back to my college days. I missed the feeling of being so young and free.

"You gonna catch our set tomorrow?" Noah asked.

"Wouldn't miss it," I said.

He pulled out more shots. "Another round." He handed them to us then held his up. "To new friends."

We tapped our shots to his. Aubrey pulled out her phone and snapped a selfie of the three of us before we said, "To new friends." We tipped back our shots and swallowed.

The word *friends* created an unexpected cavern in my chest. All my college friends were scattered around the country, and we'd lost touch after graduation since work consumed all my time. And, my colleagues at the office were just co-workers. We were cordial for business' sake, but otherwise, they weren't people I considered friends.

Usually, the knowledge that I didn't have many people I called friends didn't bother me. But for some reason, in this atmosphere, with so many people having fun and enjoying each other's company, I felt the void.

"You be sure to tell Z I took care of you two," Noah said as we stepped away from the tiki bar.

"Deal," Aubrey assured him.

"Thanks for the shots," Aubrey and I said as we twisted around.

Aubrey leaned into me as we walked. "My friend Eliza is gonna die when she sees that picture. She loves Lucid Dreams."

I laughed, knowing how cool it was in the beginning to meet famous people. The excitement wore off once you realized they were just normal people who had super cool jobs.

We made our way through groups of people playing cornhole and Can Jam as alt-rock carried over from the main stage. Aubrey joined in on a game of cornhole while I tried to get the Frisbee in the can in Can Jam. When the people playing realized I wasn't any good, they let me off the hook with a beer. I watched Aubrey sink beanbag after beanbag in her game, before we took off to see more sights.

"Aubrey," Z called from somewhere nearby.

We both stopped, searching the crowd until we spotted him sitting on top of a picnic table surrounded by a bunch of guys and girls in beach chairs. We made our way over. Someone handed him a couple of beers. He handed one to Aubrey who hopped up on the table beside him.

I reached for mine, but Z pulled it back an inch. "If I give you this, you have to promise me there is no work talk this weekend."

"Fine." I reached for it but he pulled it back again.

"You have to agree to let loose and have fun for once in your life."

I wanted to argue that I knew how to have fun, but the last five years had proven I never had fun, especially when work was involved. And Savage Beasts was work for me. "Fine."

He stifled a smile as he handed me the beer. The softening around his eyes told me he and I might just be okay again one day. I hated that I'd disappointed him. That my PR stunt caused him and Aubrey such grief. But

I couldn't undo it now. I could only move forward and *show* them I was sorry.

I cracked open my beer and stepped away from them. The sun had begun to creep toward the horizon as I took in the scene around us. It was a giant tailgate party with some of the biggest bands and singers on the planet living it up in a parking lot. I didn't get star struck easily. But it was still so damn cool to have this many famous acts in one place.

A group of guys partying beside us played beer pong under their tent.

Something inside me—likely the liquor—urged me toward them. "You need another player?" I asked.

They welcomed me over, introducing themselves as the British rock band Tri-Fold. One of them handed me the ping-pong ball. I lined it up with one of the cups and released it in a perfect arc. Swish. It dropped into the cup.

The guy next to me slapped my hand. A rush of laughter erupted from deep inside me. I felt foolish for being happy over something so stupid, but these days, happiness was hard to come by. I'd take it where I could get it.

The next hour went by in a blur. Aubrey had come by to check on me, but I assured her I was fine, playing too many games and drinking way too much beer. I threw caution to the wind—something I hadn't done in a long time. And as much fun as I was having, I knew I needed to stop drinking or I'd be puking the rest of the night. "I'm gonna take a break," I told my new friends, moving unsteadily to the edge of the tent.

A pair of big hands landed on my hips from behind. I stilled.

A hard chest pressed to my back and lips moved

beside my ear. "Having fun?" Trey asked, his lips brushing my earlobe.

A shiver rushed through my body. "Yes."

"I didn't know you were so good at beer pong."

I swallowed down my sudden nervousness. "There's a lot you don't know about me."

He chuckled, the vibration moving against my back. "What do you think all my questions have been about? I wanna know you better, Brie."

My heart thumped in my chest, loving the way his nickname for me rolled off his tongue as smooth as whiskey. But, if he'd just been trying to steady me on my feet, why were his hands still on my hips? And why did his body pressed to mine feel so right? And why in the world did he smell so damn *good?*

"What are you afraid of?" he whispered.

"I'm not afraid," I said, trying to even out the quiver in my voice.

"Bullshit."

Oh yeah? "Stop trying to keep me here to win a bet." *Ha! I'm not so oblivious after all.*

"I don't care about some stupid bet," he clipped.

I was drunk, but the certainty in his response mixed with the feel of his hands on me did crazy things to my brain. I was lonely and starved for a man's attention.

"Treyton?" a female called.

His hands dropped from my hips and he stepped away from me. The lack of contact left me feeling painstakingly bereft.

Dammit.

"Hey, Lacey," he said, the flirty timbre in his voice giving no indication that his hands were just on *my* body.

I gathered my wits about me and twisted around.

Reality was a sobering thing. Trey's hands, the one's that seconds before were groping my hips, were now wrapped around Lacey's waist and resting on her ass as she gazed up at him.

Ugh. So much for not sleeping with every girl he's with.

I moved away from the scene, cursing myself for the momentary lapse in judgment. Any guy's hands on my hips would've surely given me the same reaction.

I made my way back to my bus, my legs wobbly and my steps uneven.

"Hey," BJ said from his seat under the bus canopy.

I attempted to walk as straight as I could so he wouldn't know how much I had to drink.

"Have fun?" he asked as I dropped into the empty seat beside him.

I did have a good time. And I wouldn't let the moment with Trey spoil that. "Yup."

BJ assessed my face. "Are you drunk?"

"Why would you think I'm drunk?"

He shrugged. "You just look…different. And you smell like beer."

I dropped my chin, sniffing my shirt. Yup. Smelled like beer.

"I'm not judging you, Brielle. I think it's fantastic that you're finally loosening up."

"Finally? Let me guess. You all bet on when I'd finally loosen up too?"

"No, we didn't."

"Wouldn't put it past you."

"Brielle?"

My eyes shot up.

Aubrey stood in front of me. "Josh Temple is

performing on the main stage. You wanna go check out his set with me?"

BJ snickered beside me, probably because he was unaware Aubrey and I were now besties.

"Sure," I said, pushing myself to my feet. A wave of wooziness nearly knocked me on my ass, but I recovered. "Z doesn't wanna see the show?"

She shook her head. "He tolerates country music, but I don't really think it's his thing."

We made our way through the backstage crowd, arriving at the closed-off area beside the stage for other acts to check out the main stage without being swarmed by fans. We pushed our way as close to the stage as we could get. Aubrey instantly swayed her hips and sang along to every song Josh sang.

I didn't follow country music, but I think I needed to start. Not only was Josh hot, but he also sounded amazing. I had a feeling I'd be checking out some country playlists very soon.

Once his set ended and he made his way offstage, Aubrey turned excitedly toward me. "Let's go get a picture with him."

I laughed, probably because hanging with her made me feel like I had when I was in college. No responsibilities. No cares. Just fun. She grabbed my arm and we wove our way through the crowd.

"Give me your phone and I'll take the picture," I said.

She handed me her phone, and we waited for him to come into the backstage area where we waited. He stepped into the crowded area with his bodyguard and band, wiping his face with a towel.

"Hey," I called to him.

Josh turned our way.

"Mind if she gets a picture?" I asked.

"Not at all," he drawled, ticking his head toward the side of him.

Aubrey moved toward him. "Great show."

"Thanks," he said as he wrapped his arm around her. "Sorry, I'm sweaty."

She giggled, and I snapped a picture.

"Got it," I said.

"You don't want one?" Josh asked me as Aubrey stepped reluctantly out from under his arm.

"Oh, I…sure." I moved toward him, and Aubrey grabbed her phone from me. He wrapped his arm around me, and we smiled while Aubrey snapped the picture. "Thanks," I said, stepping away from him. "Great show out there."

He tipped his chin toward my T-shirt. "That means a lot coming from a Savage Beasts fan."

I laughed. "Yup. We have eclectic taste."

Aubrey nodded, not mentioning our connection to the band. That wasn't her style.

I gladly would've offered up that I was their publicist in case he was in need of a new one. My father had done that to me. He'd made me see dollar signs when I looked at artists. For so long I shut down the personal connection. But being on the road with the band, feeling like an outsider, had made me see that now. See that I needed acceptance. Needed to feel included. If not for the job, at least for me.

"I just posted our pictures," Aubrey said as we walked back to our buses.

"Where?"

Laughter burst out of her. "Everywhere."

* * *

I sat alone in a lawn chair outside my bus. Darkness filled the parking lot as Cankor, the night's headliner, performed on the main stage. Savage Beasts was performing tomorrow night. But they were out there watching Cankor kill their set. As were most of the other partiers. So, people were scarce around the buses.

I scrolled my emails as I chugged a big bottle of water. Drinking all day had given me a splitting headache, but the adrenaline that came with having such an unexpectedly good time had trumped it.

Anything you want to explain? A text from Keith popped up on my screen.

My brows drew in as I texted him back. **Like?**

Like why my girlfriend is hanging all over a bunch of musicians?

Aubrey and I *had* spent time taking selfies with different musicians, but I never fathomed Keith would ever find out. And even if he had, why would he care? This was the longest "conversation" we'd had in weeks.

My thumbs pressed away at my screen. **First of all, I can hang all over whoever I want.** I hit the delete button and erased that response, opting for something less bratty. **I was having a good time.**

His response was almost instantaneous. **Since when is a good time hanging all over people like some drunk college girl?**

I laughed to myself as I typed my response. **I was definitely drunk.**

I could almost hear the disdain in his voice as his words appeared. **Who are you?**

I didn't bother responding. I had a father who was controlling and cruel. I wasn't about to take it from a guy who was supposed to love me.

"You okay?"

My eyes flashed up.

Trey stood in front of me.

I craned my neck, trying to see behind him.

He twisted around to see what I was looking at, then looked back to me.

"Just looking for your little friend."

A slow smile slipped across his face.

"What?"

"You're jealous."

My nose wrinkled. "Jealous?"

"Jealous."

"As if."

"As if you're not."

I rolled my eyes. "You're drunk."

He chuckled. "I'm not even drinking."

"Why not? Everyone else is."

"I can see that." He dropped into the seat beside me.

His nearness overwhelmed me, especially after knowing what his hands felt like when they were on me. I chided my stupidity, reminding myself how quickly those hands had moved on to someone else.

A long stretch of silence passed between us as the rock music from the stage and the chants of the crowd in the distance reached us.

I had no idea why Trey was sitting there with me. Why he wasn't talking. Why he had been flirty with me and then so thoughtlessly moved on.

I didn't want to feel anything toward him. I wanted to be immune to his charm. But suddenly, he was all I could focus on. His breathing. His imposing body that seemed to touch me even though he was inches away. His tongue ring that flicked out unexpectedly, rendering my thoughts delirious.

Oh, I was definitely drunk.

"I rarely drink," Trey admitted, breaking the silence.

I snorted my disbelief.

"I'm serious, Brie. How often have you seen me drinking this entire trip?"

I shrugged. "I don't know. It's not something I pay attention to."

"Because I rarely do it."

"You're a rock star. Isn't it part of the whole scene?"

He stared up at the smattering of stars in the sky as the music continued to play in the background. "I try to stay away from things I could get addicted to."

I closed my eyes, cursing my stupidity for the second time that night. Of course he'd have a fear of addiction. He was born to an addict. And was addicted as a newborn.

"While the other guys get wasted," he continued, "I look for other things to occupy my time. I thought you realized that by now."

I dodged his eye contact, hating that I never paid enough attention to him to know that was the reason he sought female companionship. How was it that the one person responsible for keeping him in the public eye and keeping his reputation intact was turning out to be the one person who didn't really know him at all? "I never thanked you."

Trey's head hitched back. "What?"

"For being honest with me on the plane. I feel like knowing a little bit about your past makes me know you a little better now."

"Yeah?"

I nodded. "Can I ask you something else?"

"Sure."

"This is just out of total curiosity…"

"What is it, Brie?"

"Since the band hit it big and you can literally buy anything your heart desires, is there anything you still want?"

"Anything I still want?" He rubbed his hand over the day-old stubble on his chin. "Honestly?"

I nodded.

"A family."

My eyes rounded. "A family?"

He smiled. "What'd you expect me to say?"

I shrugged, loving his answer more than I should. "A big family or small family?

"Doesn't matter as long as it's mine to keep."

My chest tightened around my heart, understanding what he meant more than he knew.

Trey jolted up in his seat and strained to hear something. "Listen."

"What?"

"I love this song."

I listened, recognizing Cankor's most popular rock ballad, "Symphony." "Then why aren't you watching their set?"

He stood and extended his hand out to me. "I needed someone to dance with."

I stared at his hand, wondering how he always just knew the right thing to say. But I wasn't one of the groupies who'd do anything he asked. "I'm not dancing."

"Scared?"

My eyes lifted to his. "Of what?"

His cocky smirk slipped into place. "I think you know."

There was one thing I did know for sure. Dancing with Trey was a bad idea. I knew it with every fiber of my being. I was in a relationship—a rapidly deteriorating relationship, but a relationship nonetheless. I was lonely.

And I was starved for any kind of attention. Those combined made for some serious lapses in judgment.

I reached out my hand. Trey grasped hold of it. His grip was warm and strong as it closed over mine. A tremor rushed up my arm.

Dammit.

He yanked my hand, jerking me to my feet.

I laughed, not expecting him to be so strong.

He smiled down at me.

"What are you smiling at?" I asked.

"You never laugh."

I considered what he said and realized he was right. "I don't usually have a reason to."

His lips twisted regrettably as he gently pulled me into him. He slipped his other hand around to my lower back. The motion left a trail of numbness in its wake, and I hated that I needed the contact more than I realized. I didn't know what to do. Where to look. What to say.

Trey moved us to the song playing in the distance.

I rested my cheek against his shoulder. Was this really happening? Were Trey and I really dancing in a parking lot? His woodsy scent consumed every one of my breaths as I felt myself slowly getting lost in his embrace. He was built, sexy as hell, and he held me like he *wanted* me in his arms. And I had no idea what to do with that notion.

The soft sound of his humming filled my ears as we moved to the music. I hadn't been in anyone's arms but Keith's in over a year. This felt different. Forbidden. Risky.

"You still with your man?" Trey asked, his raspy voice sending a tremble through me.

I wondered if he felt the speeding of my heart. "Not sure."

"Why's that?"

"He saw some pictures Aubrey posted."

"He's not happy?"

"He's not happy that *I* was happy," I explained.

He scoffed.

"Well, he's not gonna ruin my fun or tell me what I can do."

"That's the Brie I know."

"Is it? Because I'm starting not to know who she is anymore."

He didn't respond, just held me tighter as he moved us to the music.

I didn't want the song to end. Didn't want him to move his arms from me. Didn't care if anyone saw us. Didn't—

The crowd roared in the distance as the song ended. *Dammit.*

I attempted to step back, but Trey held onto me. I lifted my head and met his gaze.

His eyelids were hooded, and I wanted him to keep looking at me that way. "Thanks for dancing with me, Brie."

I nodded as he stepped back, slipping out of my arms.

He buried his hands in the pockets of his jeans and stared down at the ground.

I struggled to find anything natural to do with my own arms, so I settled on crossing them.

"I'm gonna head back over to watch the rest of their set."

Awkwardness mixed with rejection swarmed my brain. "Yeah. I was just gonna go to bed anyway."

Trey's eyes cut to the bus door, and he stared at it for a long moment "Yeah, that's probably a good idea."

It was?

He looked back to me. "I don't want you out here alone. The only stragglers are drunk guys, and you know how that goes."

Inwardly, I cursed my own stupidity for the third time that night. He wanted me to be safe. He didn't want *me*. I needed to find a nice dark hole to crawl into. "Good night, Trey." I turned away from him and hurried toward the bus door where I intended to hide for the foreseeable future.

I hit the button and the door opened. I couldn't bring myself to look back at him, so I climbed the steps onto the bus and closed the door. Once I stood alone inside, concealed by the dark tinted windows, I pulled in a deep breath.

Trey turned away from the bus, having waited for me to be safely on board before heading back to the show.

What the hell was going on? How could the guy who caused me so much grief, be this totally other guy? This talented, protective, thoughtful guy? I'd known him for five years. Why now did I have to start noticing him? Why was I suddenly so confused about which way was up and which way was down when it came to him? Why now did he have to push his way into my life?

CHAPTER TEN

Brielle

I stared at the texts I'd woken up to as I ate a bowl of cereal on the bus. BJ had gotten ready before I'd even woken up, so I had the whole bus to myself. Thankfully, the tinted windows shielded me from the bright sunlight outside. It was a gorgeous day, but trying to get over my hangover would be easier without the blinding sunlight in my face.

Where are you?
What the hell, Brielle?
You need to get back to me.
Don't test me, Brielle.

It was uncanny how much Keith sounded like my father. Was I a sick person who purposely chose a guy like my father? Was I that screwed up in the head?

I tossed my phone down and went to take a shower. He didn't deserve an immediate response.

I stared in the mirror after I'd dressed in jeans and a tank top, twisting my hair into a messy knot on the top of my head for a change. I grabbed my phone, put on my dark sunglasses, and stepped off the bus.

The eighty-degree day carried zero breeze as some people prepared their areas for the day's events, while many others remained on their buses. I sat in the lawn chair outside our bus. I didn't want more texts from

Keith to spoil my day, so I called him, knowing he'd be at work and need to keep his temper in check.

"It's about fucking time," he answered.

Or not. "Hello to you, too."

"I think formalities have gone out the window since you decided to act like a goddamned teenager."

I sucked in a sharp breath.

"I mean, come on Brielle. You're off traipsing across the globe with some rock band like your life isn't here."

"Is it there, Keith? Because from where I'm sitting, you're under the impression that you can tell me what I can and can't do."

"Tell you what you can and can't do? Are you fucking serious right now?"

"I am."

He balked. "This from a girl who's been taking shit from her father her entire life?"

A cold empty silence passed between us.

"Thank you for making this easier. I'll call you once I'm back," I said.

"That's weeks away."

"Yeah. I think we can both agree we're done."

"Done?"

"I said we'll talk when I get back. I'm sorry if that's not good enough for you. Goodbye, Keith." I disconnected the call before he could say another word.

I wouldn't be my mother. I wouldn't allow a man—a man who once claimed to love me—to treat me less than I deserved. Besides, we'd been over for a while now. I guess I just needed the courage to end it.

My phone pinged and a text from Keith appeared. **I'll see you when you get back.**

I didn't respond. His words sounded like an order, and it turned my stomach. My decision had been the right one. And, *if* we saw each other when I returned, it would only be to collect whatever belongings I may have left at his condo.

Dancing with Trey made it clear to me that the spark Keith and I once had was long gone. I should have felt that electricity and pull I felt in Trey's arms with Keith. But I didn't. And I hadn't in a long time. I'd been holding on to something that was never really there.

"You okay?"

I glanced up from my phone.

Aubrey stood there.

I released a much-needed breath. "Yeah. I just told Keith we were done."

"Done?"

"Funny. That's what he said."

She snickered. "If I were a betting girl, I'd say a hot drummer with a tongue ring has something to do with it."

My suddenly wide eyes flicked around, making sure no one heard her. "What?"

She cocked her head. "I saw the two of you out here last night."

"Oh."

"Yeah. *Oh.*"

I chewed on my bottom lip.

"You don't have to say anything. But for what it's worth, I think you two would make an interesting couple."

I lifted my brows. "Interesting?"

"If the way you hate each other most days is any indication of how much you'd love each other, I think it would be freaking amazing."

I shook my head. "Nothing's going on with us."

"So, you just make a habit out of dancing in parking lots with guys you've got nothing going on with?"

I averted my gaze, having no clue what I was feeling.

"Are you sad about you and Keith?"

I glanced back to her. "Not really."

She laughed, and I couldn't help but join in.

* * *

Music from the main stage blared in the background as my beer pong buddies, Everett and Ralph, and I were at it again. Yup. I'd become a lush. This time I'd dragged Aubrey over to their tent. She and I were partners, and we were killing it—and completely drunk. We played too many games before Z appeared late in the afternoon, wrapping his arms around her and lifting her off her feet.

"Hey! We were winning," she argued, as he carried her off.

Trey stepped into her spot beside me at the table. "I'll be your partner."

I swallowed my surprise. I hadn't seen him since our dance, and I didn't know how I was supposed to act. We'd shared a nice moment, and then he all but bolted as fast as he could. Were we going to pretend it didn't happen?

Everett and Ralph, and the guys watching around the table, pounded Trey's fist, knowing who he was and loving that he'd come over to play.

Trey picked the ball out of a cup in front of us and tossed it across the table right into Everett's cup.

Everett and Ralph groaned. "Seriously? You brought a ringer?"

I looked to Trey. "Are you a ringer?"

"Is this my fact for today?" he said so only I could hear.

I cocked my head.

"I'll take that as a yes. So, yes. I'm fucking awesome at beer pong."

"And humble," I said, trying to be unfazed though the liquor coursing through my veins had me hyper-aware of his proximity.

"Not even a little bit," Trey assured me.

Everett threw the ball and it landed in a cup in front of me. I picked out the ball and downed the beer. I stacked the cup and aimed the ball across the table, sinking it in a corner cup.

"Guess I'm not the only ringer here," Trey said.

"And now you have your fact about me for today."

He shook his head. "I've got a question for you."

Ralph missed a cup and the ball bounced past us. Trey nabbed it, dunking it in the water cup before tossing it across the table. Again, he sunk the ball and flashed a smug grin my way.

I rolled my eyes as Everett drank the beer then tossed his ball into another cup in front of me. I reached for the cup, but Trey was faster, grabbing the cup, removing the ball, and downing the beer.

"I had it," I slurred. *Shit.*

"You've had a lot," he said, before sinking the ball in a cup.

I pegged him with my eyes. "Stop drinking." He didn't drink. He wasn't going to start now because of a stupid game.

"I—"

I held up my hand. "Just don't do it again."

Ralph's ball landed in a cup. I swiped the ball from it, lifted the cup, and downed the beer.

"One more cup for both of us," Everett called.

I lined up my shot and released the ball, sinking it.

Everett and Ralph groaned as Trey turned to me and wrapped his arms around me. I froze, my arms remaining at my sides. I didn't want to like the hug, but god it felt good. Trey quickly released me, probably because I didn't reciprocate the unexpected hug. Seemingly unfazed by my awkwardness, Trey turned to the guys and pounded their fists. "Thanks, guys."

My shoulders dropped. My momentary excitement deflated. Another awkward encounter. What was going on with us?

Trey glanced over his shoulder as he began to walk away. "Come on, Brie."

I said goodbye to Everett and Ralph before following alongside Trey.

"Let's take a walk around the property," he said. "See what's going on."

"In other words, you wanna sober me up?"

He laughed. "Didn't realize you were drunk."

"I'm not."

"*Riiiight.*"

I bumped him with my shoulder.

He laughed, not even missing a step. "I like seeing you have fun."

My eyes cut to his as we made our way through the backstage crowd. "Why?"

"Because you look damn hot doing it."

Excitement bubbled inside me. I hated my body for betraying me like that.

Guys slapped Trey's hand or bumped his fist as we passed by. Girls eyed him like he was something they wanted to eat. They probably did—and would if he let them.

"Are you excited for tonight?" I asked.

"Absolutely."

"You gonna stay out of trouble?" I asked.

He pressed his hand to my lower back, guiding me around a rowdy group of people. "Depends."

"On what?" I asked.

"Are you gonna get jealous again?"

"I wasn't jealous."

"You were jealous."

"You're an egotistical ass."

He chuckled.

We moved closer to the stage. Bass from a rap song pounded the pavement beneath our feet.

"So, what was it you wanted to ask me?" I said.

"What?"

"The fact. You said my beer pong skills couldn't be my fact."

He stifled a smile.

"Oh, God. What is it?"

He laughed. "Why'd you say it like that?"

"I know you."

His eyes flashed down, and for the first time ever, I saw an instance of vulnerability I'd never seen in Trey before. It was beautiful. He was beautiful.

"Brielle?" a gruff voice called.

Trey and I both twisted around.

A guy I recognized from our video call walked toward us. The video did not do the train wreck justice. His sagging jeans, too-tight wife beater T-shirt, and chunky gold chains were almost comical if they weren't his everyday attire. He walked—make that strutted—toward me with outstretched arms. "What's up, girl?"

Embarrassment filled me as Flow Houz wrapped his arms around me. If I thought my hug with Trey was awkward, this hug was a hundred times more awkward. "Hey, Flow."

He stepped out of the awkward semi-hug and turned to Trey, extending his fist to him. "Sup, homes?"

Trey reciprocated, though amusement played across his face. "Sup."

Flow looked to me. "Girl, that spin you did for me was pure magic. I don't know how to thank you."

"All part of my job," I said.

He draped his arm over my shoulders, clearly not understanding that I wasn't touchy-feely with my clients. "Come on. I want you to meet my crew."

I glanced to Trey, pleading with my eyes for him to save me, but he just held up his hands and smiled, enjoying my mortification way too much.

"I'll catch you later, Brielle," Trey said, using my full name and acting as if he hadn't just been about to ask me something—something I really wanted to hear.

"Later, homes," Flow said, pulling me to the opposite side of the grounds. "Girl, I can't wait to talk more about branding and the merch I plan to sell. With your help, I'z about to blow up."

I let him pull me toward his crew, though something a lot more appealing was walking in the other direction.

CHAPTER ELEVEN

Treyton

Night cast a shadow of darkness over the stage as we took our spots behind our instruments. The excitement was palpable as the crowd roared on the other side of the huge black sheet hung in front of the stage to obstruct their view of us until we dropped it.

Z glanced to me and I counted down, banging my sticks three times before our music blasted through the massive outdoor arena. I didn't think the crowd could get any louder, but once the sheet dropped, they became a boom of thunder, erupting at the sight of us. But the sight of them—all one hundred thousand swaying bodies—was just as invigorating to us.

Z broke into the lyrics to "Midnight," and the entire arena sang along. We used to end with "Midnight," but since it was such a crowd favorite, we'd been opening with it to really get the overseas fans pumped.

I pounded away at my drums, glancing to the designated artists' area where we watched various acts over the past two days. There wasn't a free spot. Everyone we'd been partying with had filled the space, wanting to hear us play. It was a rush to have them looking up to us.

Our set was the most explosive I'd seen over the weekend and everyone knew it. From pyrotechnics to our mega screen, we brought it. The other artists would get to our level someday if they put in the blood, sweat, and tears we had. We weren't an overnight success. But once we hit it big, the sky was the limit.

Once we finished "Midnight," Z introduced the rest of us to the crowd while he drank some water and moved across the front of the stage. He and I had come a long way from our time in foster care. We both thanked our lucky stars every day that we came out on top. We definitely found each other at the right time. Who knew what would've happened if we hadn't found each other or music.

"Give it up for the best mother fucking drummer on the planet!" Z yelled.

The crowd roared as I broke into my drum solo, beating the hell out of my drum set. I could feel the bass drum like an extension of my heartbeat as I let the sticks control me. I finished as strong as I'd started, lifting my sticks high in the air to the roar of the crowd. It never got old. *Never.*

Z shook his head, amused by my need to show off when given the chance.

As he proceeded to introduce Camden and Marcus, giving them their individual moments to shine, I glanced to the side of the stage where BJ and Aubrey stood. My eyes searched the area. Where was Brie? I hadn't seen her since she took off with the Eminem wannabe. The guy was such a tool. I actually felt bad she needed to represent him.

An unfamiliar throbbing began in my chest, as my mind whirled with the possibilities. She hadn't missed one of our shows since she'd been on the road with us. Where the hell was she? I craned my neck, trying to nab Aubrey's eyes.

She saw me, and her eyes narrowed in confusion.

"Where's Brielle?" I mouthed, knowing she never ventured far from the side of the stage while we performed.

She shrugged, glancing to BJ and asking the same question. He too shrugged, glancing over his shoulder but coming up short.

The throbbing in my chest intensified. "Call her," I mouthed to both of them.

They nodded, as our next song "Sleepless" began. My attention returned to the song. Since I could play the drums with my eyes closed, I had no trouble searching the crowd of artists packed into the side area as I pounded away at my set. Had Brie somehow ended up there and not with our team backstage? I spotted lots of familiar faces, but none of them were her or the rapper.

While I wanted to enjoy all the love we were receiving from the Hungarian fans, as well as the other musicians, time dragged on and Brie still hadn't appeared. I'd never wanted to be offstage as much as I did in that moment. Song after song, I waited. But still no Brie. As soon as Z said goodnight, I abandoned my drums and flew backstage. "Did you get a hold of her?" I asked Aubrey.

"She didn't answer," she said.

"She's probably just on the bus. She had a lot to drink today," BJ added.

He was right. She had been drinking all day. And for someone who didn't drink like that, it would've eventually caught up with her. But if she wasn't on the bus? I shook off the thought, not allowing my mind to go there.

I made my way back toward the buses. People slapped my back and greeted me as I passed. I tried not to be rude, but I could see our buses and needed to be there. The weirdness of the situation was not lost on me. I never had to worry about anyone but my own ass. Now, I was worried about someone who despised me most of the time. I quickened my pace, needing to see with my own eyes that she was okay so the clanging in my chest would return to normal.

"Hey, rock star."

I spun toward the cringe-worthy voice and found her rapper moving toward me. My eyes shot around him, but Brielle wasn't there. "Where is she?"

"Who?"

"Brielle. I haven't seen her since she took off with you."

A slow smirk swept across his lips.

"Dude, don't mess with me right now," I warned, about ready to lose my shit. "Either you know where she is or you don't."

"She didn't mention you were her man," he said, his eyes drifting over my torn jeans and sleeveless T-shirt.

"I'm not."

His brows, both with shave marks cut through them, lifted. "But you wanna be."

My lip curled into a snarl.

"What is it you like about her? Her nice juicy rack or her perfect ripe ass?"

The hair on the back of my neck stood on end.

"Don't keep her on ice, bro," he persisted. "If I have it my way, I'll be the one breaking down her back door and havin' some dirty face time with her puss—"

My fist connected with his jaw before he could say one more thing about Brie. It caught him off guard and he stumbled back. But for a scrappy wannabe rapper, he didn't go down like I thought he would. He came back at me, his fist connecting with my left eye before I could block it. Instinctively, my hand shot to my eye, which gave him time to lower his head and drive into my stomach with a roar. I staggered back with his head in my gut, slamming into someone's table and sending the contents crashing behind me. I grabbed him in a headlock. My fist came up, hammering him with upper-cuts.

Muffled shouting around us registered as multiple arms wrapped around me, pulling me off him.

"Calm down, man," Z said as he and Reggie pulled me off the punk.

"He attacked me," the rapper shouted, blood dripping from his nose as people pulled him away from me.

"Fuck you," I said, spitting on the ground.

"I will sue you, bro. Sue you for everything you've got," he yelled.

"I'd love to see you try."

"Trey?" Brie stepped through the crowd that had gathered.

A relieved breath whooshed out of me. *She's all right.*

Her eyes jumped between me and the rapper, trying to discern what happened. Then, without warning, her features hardened and her narrowed eyes shot daggers into mine. "What did you do?"

I blinked back my shock. "What did *I* do?"

She huffed. "You just couldn't stay out of trouble, could you?"

Was she seriously blaming *me?*

Her disgusted glare reminded me of all the times she'd found me in precarious situations before. But this time it wasn't about me. It was about *her*. I was defending *her* fucking honor.

She turned away and hurried over to the rapper, making sure he was okay while his crew moved him back to their buses. She trailed them, a pathetic follower chasing after a new paycheck.

Z pulled me away, shoving me toward our buses. "What the hell is wrong with you?"

"You too?" I snapped, stunned he'd take anyone's side but mine.

"What does *that* mean?"

"You just assume it was me." I dropped into a lawn chair outside the bus I shared with Cam and Marcus. "You know me better than that."

He crossed his arms and rested his ass on a table, glaring down at me. "You're not making any sense."

BJ appeared with Camden and Marcus. "What the hell's going on?"

"We need a minute," Z said to them. "Can you hang in the bus?"

Sensing Z's seriousness, they walked onto the bus.

"Hey," Cam called, sticking his head out and tossing me a cold can of beer. "Put that on your eye."

I lifted the can to my eye, and a long stretch of silence passed between Z and me. Once he was sure no one was within earshot, he leveled me with his eyes. "Talk."

"He said some inappropriate things about Brielle."

Z's head shot back, unprepared for the reason I pounced on the rapper.

"She's his publicist now," I explained. "So, hearing him disrespect her made me think it's only a matter of time before he tries something, and I couldn't let that happen."

"You need to tell her."

"No," I snapped. She'd taken his side and accused *me* of starting it. "You won't tell her either," I warned Z.

He held up his hands. "Not my business. But if you're

really worried about her well-being, you need to give her a heads up about him."

"You've got a hell of a lot of explaining to do." Brielle stormed over with her fists clenched by her side.

The sight of her tightened a knot in my gut. She hadn't trusted me, yet she was looking to me for an explanation. *Make up your damn mind, traitor.*

Z disappeared onto the bus.

"Talk, Trey," she demanded.

I lowered the beer can from my eye, but said nothing.

She dug her hands into her hips and shot me those condescending eyes she was so good at. "You're not gonna talk?"

"Why bother? That asshole probably filled you in."

"He said you attacked him for no reason."

"Oh, yeah. That sounds like me."

She crossed her arms and said nothing.

"Tell me you don't believe that."

"I'm so confused who the real Treyton Collins is right now. My head is literally spinning."

"You didn't answer my question. Do *you* think that sounds like me?"

Her eyes averted mine. "I don't know."

I stood up and moved forward until I was in front of her. She tipped her head back to see my face and her breath caught in her throat. I glared down at her, ignoring the way her body reacted to mine. My nostrils flared as I held back everything I really wanted to say. "Good luck spinning this one." I stepped around her and climbed onto my bus.

She and the rapper would be great together. Both of them had being assholes down to a science.

CHAPTER TWELVE

Brielle

"You better clean this shit up, Brielle," my father yelled through the phone. "I've got Arthur ready to fly out there and do it for you if you can't handle it."

"I'll handle it." I disconnected the call, knowing I needed to do something now that videos of the fight had surfaced—less than an hour after it occurred.

For once in my career, I didn't know what the hell to do. I'd been trying to sleep off the alcohol so I could watch the guys perform. When I woke up, I'd not only broken my rule about drinking on the job, but I'd also missed their entire set. I wanted to at least be there when they got offstage. That's when all hell broke loose.

What made the whole scene even more infuriating was that I didn't get a straight answer. Flow was a tool who I didn't know, and I wouldn't have been caught dead spending time with him had I not been representing him. He swore Trey just attacked him for no reason—which made no sense.

And Trey? Trey made a habit of screwing up. And as much as his behavior normally drove me crazy, I wanted to believe him this time. I wanted to have *his* back. But he was giving me nothing.

There was one thing I was certain about. The anger in Trey's eyes when I didn't believe him. *That* was real.

There was a knock on my bus door. It was nearly one in the morning, so I had no clue who I'd find out there. I dragged in a deep breath and pushed myself to my feet, knowing I needed to face whomever it was eventually. My breath released when I found Aubrey standing outside alone. I pushed open the door.

"Got a minute?" she asked, her eyes scanning the area around her as if she didn't want anyone seeing her at my bus.

I stepped back, and she climbed inside.

My phone rang, and I checked the screen. My father again. I powered off my phone and tossed it on the table. "Sit."

Aubrey sat and looked up at me, her eyes plagued with indecision. "What are you gonna do?"

"What do you mean?"

She cocked her head. "You represent both of them, but one of them has to be the bad guy. Who's it gonna be?"

"Did Trey send you in here?"

Her nose wrinkled. "What? No."

"Be real with me, Aubrey."

"The way I see it, I'm one of your only friends out here. If anyone's gonna be real with you, it's me."

"We're friends?" I asked, taken aback by her words.

"After being together every day for over a month, I'd hope so."

A burst of warmth spread through my chest—a feeling I really needed at a time like that.

"So, my question is, are you gonna throw Treyton under the bus to protect your new golden boy?"

"He's not my golden boy," I assured her, knowing my father probably gave me the moron to watch me lose my mind.

"Doesn't matter," Aubrey continued. "The guys will never forgive you if you hurt Treyton. You have the chance not to. What are you gonna do?"

I dropped into the seat beside her. "I have no idea how to spin this one."

"Do you know why Treyton fought him?"

I shook my head. "He just said I should know him better than that."

"And what do *you* think?"

"I think he's screwed up more times than I can count over the last five years."

"Recently?"

I considered her question. Over the past few weeks, he'd actually given me more reasons to trust him than not to trust him. I shook my head.

Aubrey's eyes lowered to her cowboy boots, and she released a sigh.

"What aren't you saying?" I asked.

She didn't meet my gaze. "I will deny this if it comes back to me."

"What?"

"I heard Z tell Cam there's more to it, but it's not his place to say."

"What's that even mean?"

Her eyes cut to mine as she shrugged. "That's all I heard. I think you need to find out the truth before you do something you might regret." She stood and walked to the door, disappearing into the darkness outside.

I dropped my face into my palms. Why the hell had Trey done it? What hadn't he told me? I wanted to believe him, but what was I supposed to do when he wouldn't tell me the truth?

Trey and Flow—two guys in the public eye—fighting at a music festival in front of hundreds of people would be fodder for late night talk shows and gifs for years to come if I didn't make this right. Not to mention my father was ready to replace me as their publicist as soon as I failed.

If only I knew the truth.

I stood and moved to the door. It was late, and the crowds outside had thinned. A heaviness weighed on me as I walked to the bus beside mine. I sobered my features, straightened my spine, and knocked on the door. I stepped back once it opened and Camden stood there, his green eyes narrowed and boring into mine. "Yeah?"

"Where's Treyton?"

"I don't think he's got anything to say to you."

"Do I look like that will stop me?"

He scoffed, almost amused by my I-don't-give-a-shit attitude.

"I hope you're decent, boys," I called, pushing by Cam and climbing onto the bus.

Marcus played the guitar beside BJ, who clearly was on their bus to avoid me on our bus.

My eyes jumped around the bus. "Where is he?"

"You sure you wanna do this right now?" BJ asked.

I cocked my head.

Knowing I wasn't one to give up that easily, he ticked his head toward the back of the bus.

"You mind giving us a couple of minutes?" It wasn't a question.

BJ, Marcus, and Cam begrudgingly made their way to the door and off the bus, closing the door behind them.

My lungs expanded on a long, deep breath as I stalked down the short hallway. Of course, Trey took the bed in the back and made Marcus and Cam take the bunks. I didn't bother knocking. I just threw the door open.

Trey nearly jumped off his bed where he'd been

sprawled out in only his boxers. "Jesus Christ, Brie. I could've had a girl in here!"

"So?"

"I could've been jerking off?"

"And?"

He shook his head, unamused by my nonchalance or my appearance in his bedroom.

"We need to talk."

He stood up and I stepped back. His height was imposing in such close quarters, not to mention his bare chest in my face.

"I think we've said all that needs to be said." His tone was flat and his eyes cold.

"I'll say when we've said enough."

He hitched a brow. "Careful, Brie. You work for us."

I ignored his threat. "I want the truth."

He scoffed. "Why? You already took his side."

I jammed my index finger into his chest. "Whose side I want to take is *yours*, you stubborn ass."

He grabbed my hand against his chest and held onto it there. "Why? Why do you want to take *my* side?"

My eyes pled with him to stop questioning me, but it didn't stop my pulse from slamming into the wall of my chest. Could he feel it?

He loosened his grip, but instead of letting go, he laced our fingers together. "Why, Brie?"

A shiver coasted over my body. I tried to ignore it. "Why'd you fight him, Trey?"

He shook his head.

Between our close proximity and the fact that he was holding my hand, my heart had become a jackhammer close to breaking free. He had to feel it. "Tell me."

His eyes lowered, studying my lips with careful appraisal. "I was doing the right thing for once in my life."

"The right thing for who?"

"Someone I care about…" His eyes lifted to mine. "More than I should."

I swallowed hard. "You're talking in riddles."

He chewed his bottom lip, clearly stalling so he didn't have to answer my questions.

"If you're not going to tell me the truth—" I turned to leave, but he didn't release my hand, pulling me back into his chest.

I stared up into his blue eyes, waiting him out.

He was the one who'd pulled *me* back but now he looked conflicted over it. His eyes darted away from mine and his jaw ticked. "He said some things about you."

"What kind of things?"

His eyes cut back to mine. "Things a man does not say about his publicist."

"I work in a man's world, Trey. I can handle guys being guys."

He closed his eyes as if it pained him to hear me say that. "God dammit, Brie. You shouldn't have to."

My eyes rounded.

"Your client said he planned to do filthy things to you."

My tough façade faltered. "He said that?"

"He said that. And I needed to be sure he knew if he disrespected you, he'd have to deal with me."

Every part of my body stilled as a knot inched up the back of my throat. Trey had been looking out for *me*.

"But what did you do?" he said. "You took his side."

"You didn't tell me what he said." It sounded so pathetic now.

"I shouldn't have *had* to."

Trey had been standing up for me. *I* was the someone he cared about who he shouldn't. I was the one who he was protecting. I was the one who screwed up. Not him. *Dammit.*

Tears stung my eyes. I blinked them back. I would not cry.

Trey tilted his head, his eyes assessing mine—obviously noticing my bravado wavering. He slanted his head forward.

I held my breath.

He inched closer.

Our mouths were dangerously close. I could feel his breath, and I couldn't tear my eyes away from his lips.

"You need to leave, Brie," he said.

I blinked, my words a mere whisper. "What?"

"You got your answer. Now you need to leave."

I sucked in a sharp breath as my eyes lifted to his.

His were narrowed coldly as he dropped my hand and stepped back. "I shouldn't have had to tell you. You should've trusted me."

I threw my hands out to my sides—embarrassed, frustrated, and *pissed.* "Right. Because you've given me so many reasons to trust you."

His voice lowered. "That right there is why you need to get off my bus."

Heat pulsed in my cheeks as I spun away from him and stormed down the short hallway to the door. I shoved it open, unable to get off his bus fast enough. Between my embarrassment, shock, and anger, I didn't know who was the bigger asshole.

Him or me?

CHAPTER THIRTEEN

Treyton

Drum it up to a misunderstanding…

Sources at the scene of the Hungarian music festival fight say Treyton Collins, drummer for the rock band Savage Beasts, misheard up-and-coming rapper Flow Houz when he complimented their shared publicist. That's all it took for Collins to go to battle. "It was a huge misunderstanding," a source close to the rapper said. "Both men agreed to move on from it and shook hands for good measure." "There was a lot of drinking and testosterone flying at the festival," an onlooker said. "No harm, no foul. We're all just here for the music."

I stared down at the words on my phone the following morning as I lay in bed on the bus, feeling foolish for believing for one second that Brie wasn't a conniving bitch who spun stories and used people to do it. I saw the way she spun the fight. I saw the word *misunderstanding* tossed around because *she'd* put it out there, claiming *I* misunderstood that asshole.

I didn't give a fuck that people saw me punch that fool. The world needed to know the way he talked about women. The way he assumed all women were objects and only good for one thing. Too many of these guys used women in their videos and as topics for their lyrics, disrespecting them in ways I'm not even sure the women realized. That's why I'd been honest with Brie—omitting his crude words to spare her embarrassment.

What pissed me off was she *knew* he'd disrespected her, but still made it look like a misunderstanding. That's why guys like him got away with the things they did. The Brie I thought I knew would've called a guy out on that shit. But what did she do? She played Switzerland so she could have her cake and eat it too.

I guess the wannabe rapper's paycheck was more important than her self-respect. Or me.

Brielle

I was thrilled to be leaving Hungary when our bus caravan departed the concert grounds around 8 p.m. the following night. I stayed on my bus that day, wanting to keep my distance from everyone after what happened the previous night.

We drove through the night en route to Austria. We were spending our day off there before arriving in Munich for two concerts. I sat at the small table, my cell phone casting the only light in the bus. It was midnight somewhere near Austria, which meant it was around 3 p.m. in California. I sent off a text to Irene, the office secretary, hoping she hadn't left yet. **Send Flow Houz a disengagement letter.**

I popped M&M's into my mouth as I waited. My foot bounced restlessly beneath me, hoping Irene texted me back sooner rather than later. And, hopefully, it wasn't *after* she ran to my father. Irene had worked for him since he began Artists Limited. She was a mother figure to him, though she still feared him like most did.

My phone pinged. **Your father will never agree to that.**

Regardless of her loyalty to my father, I was never working with Flow again. What Trey told me he'd said pissed me off. I'd worked hard to be taken seriously in the entertainment industry. Some wannabe rapper wasn't going to disrespect me by assuming I wasn't a true professional.

My anger fueled my fingers. **Then send him a termination of services letter from me. Arthur can have him.** Arthur was a leech. He'd grab onto any artist if he thought it would benefit him. He had no morals and could justify representing anyone. In his eyes a sexist perv wasn't a murderer, so what was the big deal?

You sure about this? Irene texted back.

I knew handling it via text showed weakness, but it was so much easier than dealing with my father who'd surely tell me to suck it up, without concern for what Flow had said about me. **Absolutely.**

* * *

I gazed out the bus window at the Austrian hotel, an actual castle. It was a little before two in the morning, but even through the darkness, the view was exquisite. I couldn't wait to explore the castle with its towers, wooden doors, gothic style windows, and sprawling property.

"Maybe you should hang back," BJ said, walking out from his room in the back of the bus with a small suitcase. "I'm going to get the guys checked in first."

I nodded, watching him exit the bus and walk into the hotel.

BJ always checked the guys in so they could go right up to their rooms without being seen.

I waited, watching out the window. Z, giving Aubrey a piggyback ride, escorted by Reggie, made their way into the hotel a short while later. I wondered if they'd seen the news story. Wondered if Aubrey thought I did the right thing.

Camden, Marcus, and Trey stepped off their bus. I pulled back so they couldn't see my silhouette through the tinted windows. Trey's head hung down as he walked, clutching the straps of his backpack.

I waited a few minutes before checking myself in. While I waited for my keycard, I glanced around the lobby at the old wall tapestries, high ceilings, and elaborate chandeliers. Then I noticed the piano to the right. My chest constricted, knowing Trey would've spotted it too.

With my keycard in hand, I moved through the lobby and rode the elevator to the fifth floor. I followed the sign toward room 525, checking the small golden plaque beside each door as I walked. A door to my left flew open and Trey stepped out into the hallway causing me to jack up.

He stopped short, startled by me standing there. We stared at each other for no more than a couple of seconds before he stepped around me and walked down the hallway.

A knot formed in my stomach. How could he be *that* angry with me? How could he think I'd throw *him* under the bus over some stranger? Hadn't he seen the news story?

I wanted to follow him and demand he talk to me, but I'd done that in Hungary and it ended in an epic fail with me being kicked off his bus. I heaved a sigh. If he wanted to speak to me, he would.

I finally found my room and jumped right into bed. After a few hours of tossing and turning, daylight arrived. I showered and dressed in sneakers and clothes for hiking. I'd scheduled myself on *The Sound of Music* tour weeks ago, eager to see all the places where they filmed the movie. Now, starved for sleep, I wasn't as eager.

I hurried through the hotel lobby to meet my group. I spotted the band laughing and all geared up for their own excursion—one I clearly hadn't been invited on. I tried to ignore the disappointment stewing within me, but it sucked that for a fleeting moment, I felt included and part of the group. Within seconds, all of that had been ripped away. And I had no one to blame but myself. I'd jumped to conclusions. I'd turned my back on someone I was just beginning to know better and understand. What did I expect?

I spotted the woman in the lederhosen holding *The Sound of Music* sign beside a white van. I climbed into the van filled with excited families en route to Salzburg where we'd board our tour bus. As we drove through the picturesque Austrian streets, I tried to lose myself in the movie soundtrack playing inside the van. But trying to lose myself and actually doing it were two totally different things.

* * *

I hobbled into the hotel six hours later as the sun had already begun to set. My feet ached from all the walking across Salzburg. But I'd be lying if I said I didn't enjoy seeing all the locations in the film: The garden and fountain where Maria and the kids danced. The convent. The Von Trapp's house where most of the movie took place. The gazebo where Liesl jumped from bench to bench and Maria kissed the captain. And the church where they were married. It was a magical day.

But now, back at the hotel, I felt alone. I had no family who checked in on me. No friends who just wanted to say hello. And no one to even eat with. I needed to leave. Not for my father but because I didn't want to be there anymore.

Munich *would* be my last stop.

CHAPTER FOURTEEN

Brielle

Our three-bus caravan pulled into the concert venue in Munich a few hours before the band's first show. After sound check, I made sure the meet and greet area backstage was ready before greeting the lucky fans who'd won the opportunity to meet the band.

The guys filed into the room and took their spots in front of the concert venue's backdrop. Not one of them even acknowledged I was there. Hadn't they seen the story? Hadn't they realized I didn't place the blame on anyone? Their reactions definitely affirmed my decision to leave the tour.

I walked to the hallway where the fans were waiting impatiently. Their smiles beamed once I entered, knowing I was what stood between them and the band. "Hi, everyone. You ready to meet the guys?"

They screamed, some of the girls breaking into tears.

"Okay. Just a few rules," I said. "Two at a time. Say your hellos then work your way to the open spots between the guys. You can take a selfie or have me take your photo."

They were all nodding their understanding as their eyes jumped eagerly between me and the door.

"Okay, let's get started." I pointed to the two girls in front wearing the matching Z T-shirts. "You two are up first."

They squealed, nearly bouncing out of their shoes.

I escorted them into the room. They practically jumped into Z's arms. Poor Aubrey. It was a good thing she was secure in their relationship because the women loved Z. The girls greeted the rest of the guys then one of them handed me her phone before snuggling in between Z and Trey.

"Ready?" I asked, holding her phone up so I could get them all into the picture. "Smile." I couldn't help looking at Trey through the screen. He didn't smile. Was he purposely being defiant because I'd asked them to smile?

The girls said their goodbyes, retrieving their phone from me before the next two people, a wife and husband, hurried into the room. The woman handed me her phone before greeting the guys. Once they talked to them for a few minutes about the tour, they stood amongst them. "Okay, smile," I said, getting them all into the picture. Again, Trey didn't smile.

The remainder of the meet and greets continued that way. Me taking pictures and Trey not smiling. That was completely unlike him since he was the fun-loving member of the band who usually made every fan feel comfortable.

Once the last two fans left, the guys walked toward the door, eager to get ready to take the stage.

"Treyton," I called with conviction in my tone.

The guys all mumbled as they walked out of the room with Trey trailing behind them.

Son of a bitch.

I stormed out of the room, stalking backstage where everyone grabbed food or drinks. I walked right up to Trey whose back was to me and stepped in front of him. "You heard me."

His brows squished together.

"You're acting like a child. Act like a man."

The way the room fell silent told me all eyes were on us, but my eyes were only on Trey.

He grabbed my arm roughly and pulled me toward a door on the far side of the room. My feet fought to keep up as he moved us through the door and into a hallway, slamming the door behind us.

I expected him to yell at me.

To glare at me.

To fire me.

But instead, he walked into me so I needed to step back, right into the wall.

He caged me in, his hands pressing to the wall above my head. And just like he had the other night on his bus, he slanted his head so our faces were close. "Fuck me?" he asked, the deep timbre in his voice menacing.

I swallowed hard. Having him that close was daunting, especially with him pissed at me and me even more pissed at him. I remained focused and angry. Because I was. How dare he ignore me?

He shifted his hips, his unexpected erection pressing into my stomach. "Does a child feel like this?"

Though the intrusion sent zingers through me, I couldn't let that distract me. "Stop."

"Stop what?"

"Stop using your body to try to make me lose focus."

He smirked with an evil glint in his eyes. "Is that what I do to you?"

"No, you piss me off."

"See, you keep saying things like that, but I'm starting to see it as a defense mechanism. One that helps you stay away from me."

"You're the one staying away from *me*. You're the one who just ignored me back there. You're the one who threw me off your bus. You're the one who made sure I was *not* included today."

He growled. "Because you ruined everything."

"*I* ruined everything?"

"I thought we were making progress. I thought we turned a corner. Then you went and fucked it up with that ridiculous news statement."

"What did you want from me? You sucker-punched my client."

"Your client was admiring your tits and ass. But you made it look like *I* misunderstood *him*."

"I—"

"Fucked. Everything. Up."

His words, mixed with my embarrassment over not having his back from the start, made my blood boil. He was *not* going to pin it all on me. I glared into his eyes, trying to feel the same disgust I'd felt so many times before when I looked at him. He could have *told* me. He could have made me see he was protecting me from Flow in the first place. Now, he was knocking my attempt to clean it up.

I straightened my spine. "I'm always cleaning up after *you*. I could make you look like the manwhore people think you are. I could let the tabloids run with pictures of you with every female you've ever been seen with. I could let them post stories they've embellished about you, but I don't. I call them misunderstandings. And what do you do the second you don't want to hear something was a misunderstanding? You turn your back on me."

I lifted my hands and shoved him away from me.

He stumbled back a couple of feet, not expecting my reaction. I watched his chest rise and fall, but he said nothing.

"Go play your drums and sleep with some groupie. And whether you like it or not, when it hits the press, I'll be sure to call it a misunderstanding." I moved away from him and began down the hallway. "Oh, and if you would've let me finish," I called over my shoulder. "You would've known I terminated my contract with my client." I pushed open the exit door at the end of the hall with as much vigor as I'd pushed Trey away from me with. I stepped through it without giving him, or anyone else who might have stumbled upon our confrontation, a second glance.

CHAPTER FIFTEEN

Treyton

I pounded away at my drums as the sea of Munich fans chanted and swayed along to the chorus of "Crossover." It was easy to be swept up in the madness in the outdoor venue. Swept up in the love these fans had for our band. Swept up in the cell phone lights creating their very own star-filled sky. But seeing Brie so thoroughly pissed weighed heavily on my mind.

It wasn't that I hadn't seen—or *made*—Brie pissed before. It was that I could see the hurt behind the anger.

Or, maybe it was *my* hurt behind *my* anger.

Who the fuck knew?

What I did know was this constant tension with her was driving me nuts. It wasn't healthy to feel so much animosity toward someone, but at the same time feel so disappointed in them as well.

It couldn't just be that she'd taken the rapper's side over mine. It couldn't just be that she'd disrespected herself by keeping him on as a client. It couldn't just be that I cared that much about her pinning the fight on me in the news. It had to be something else. And the fact that I couldn't shake the uneasy feeling pissed me the hell off.

Once the show ended and we headed backstage, my eyes wandered around the room. The guys spoke to some VIPs while BJ grabbed a drink. No one else was around.

"She already left," BJ called to me.

"Who?"

"Brielle. It's who you were looking for, right?"

"No," I lied.

But as I took off for the bus, I wondered if the person I'd really been lying to was myself.

* * *

After returning to the hotel, I showered and ordered room service, but the walls around me began to close in. I abandoned my food and pulled on a T-shirt to go with the basketball shorts I already wore. I grabbed my keycard and headed to the lobby.

The place was empty and the piano called my name. I walked to it, running my hand over the smooth ebony surface before sitting on the bench seat. I pushed open the cover and my fingers floated over the keys.

My mom loved it when I played for her. It's probably why I'd been getting the urge lately to play. An emptiness in my chest was keeping me up at night. And it was telling me that something was missing in my life. Something all the groupies in the world, all the fame in the world, and all the money in the world wouldn't fill. Despite the fact that I only had my adoptive parents for ten years, I missed having people watching over me. Missed having people loving me wholeheartedly. Missed having people I could talk to about my highs and lows.

I hadn't lied when I'd told Brie family was the one thing money couldn't buy. It was the one thing I knew I needed to make me feel whole.

My mom's favorite song "Clair de Lune" materialized from my fingers, something that had been happening a lot lately. I closed my eyes. I could almost see her beside me beaming with pride as my nine-year-old self played the song she loved so much. There were days when tears would trail down her cheeks as I played it, and I wondered what memories the song elicited that she didn't divulge to me. Had it been tough raising me? Had it been tough keeping a brave face once she got ill?

"Stop playing that."

My eyes sprang open but my fingers continued moving over the keys.

Brielle, with her hands on her hips, replaced the vision of my mother. "Stop playing that song," she repeated.

My brows pushed together, both irritated by her presence and confused by her request. What did she care what I played? "Why?"

"Because I don't like it."

"Why not? It's a beautiful piece."

"Not to me." Too many emotions played across her face as she stared me in the eyes.

"Why is honesty so difficult for you?" I asked.

Her teeth clenched and her jaw tightened.

Game on. I could wait her out all day.

But, our standoff didn't last that long. She huffed and took off, leaving me to the quiet of the lobby and the solace of my song.

"*Dammit*," I cursed under my breath. She may have been able to play the asshole card for extended lengths of time, but that wasn't me. I knew when enough was enough. I stopped playing the song, glancing over to where she headed.

Her steps faltered when she realized I'd stopped playing. But, in true Brie fashion, she kept moving to the elevators.

I sat there for a long time after she disappeared. And the only thing I could come up with, the only thing that made sense moving forward, was that something had to give.

CHAPTER SIXTEEN

Brielle

The last place I wanted to be was the front seat of a passenger van winding through the picturesque mountains of Belgium. I expected to be on the first flight out of Munich. But then I got the confirmation for the band's zip lining adventure that I'd arranged a month ago. I'd initially thought a day of zip lining would be a great photo op. But now, with Trey and me at odds and Aubrey and BJ deciding to hang back at the hotel, I felt like a third wheel.

We hit a bump in the dirt mountain road and the guys bounced in the rows behind me. Of course I didn't turn to look. No chance I wanted to risk making eye contact with Trey after yet another stellar encounter by the piano.

The driver pulled to a stop at a building that resembled a cabin. Someone threw the side door open, and the band piled out.

I gathered the cameras I'd gotten for the guys to secure to their helmets to record their rides. I pulled in a deep cleansing breath and stepped outside into the seventy-degree day. Puffy white clouds that looked close enough to touch filled the sky. Lush green forest stretched as far as the eye could see. There was no doubt the guys would be capturing a breath-taking adventure.

"Hey, I'm Jay," a guy who stepped out of the cabin said. "Welcome to Zip Line Adventures. I'll be one of your guides today along with Hans and Bryce."

The guys greeted Jay, shaking his hand and introducing themselves.

I approached Z with a camera. "Here you go."

Z took it, examining the small camera.

"Remember, record your rides and turn so you can get the guys going behind you."

I handed a camera to Cam. "Be sure to watch your mouth since these pick up audio too, and you want everything appropriate for *all* your fans."

"So 'fuck yeah' is off-limits?" Cam asked.

Marcus laughed as I handed him a camera and cocked my head at Cam. "Just be real. You're trying to give fans a glimpse into a day in the life of Savage Beasts." I glanced around, looking for Trey who'd disappeared—or was avoiding me. I handed the extra camera to Marcus. "Here. Be sure Treyton gets this."

"You're not coming?" Marcus asked.

"Nope. I'll be recording you guys leaving and will meet you at the bottom to get you returning."

"Bit of a problem with that," Jay said. "Only way down are those lines." He ticked his chin toward the first set of zip lines.

"Nope. I'm riding back down in that." I glanced toward the empty spot where the van we'd come in had been parked.

Shit.

"Our ride meets us at the bottom," Jay explained.

My pulse began to pound in my ears. This wasn't happening. I couldn't zip line. I was terrified of heights. My knees began to shake beneath me.

"What's wrong, Brielle?" Trey asked, stepping out of the cabin. "You love heights. The higher the better," he said, using my own lie to taunt me.

I pulled in a breath and steeled my features before turning toward him. "Yes, but this is *your* trip. You don't need me tagging along. Guys only."

"I think we can make an exception," Trey said. "Right, guys?"

The guys all mumbled a comment as Jay and Hans secured helmets onto their heads and helped them into their harnesses.

I walked toward the cabin, hoping someone inside could call me a ride.

Trey stepped in front of me, stopping me. "The first line starts there." He pointed toward the platform. "You're gonna need a helmet and harness."

I glared at him. "You're loving this, aren't you?"

His lips slipped into a smirk. "All you've gotta do is be honest."

My mind reeled, trying to think of a way out of it. But if I backed down, he won. And the last thing I was gonna do was let Treyton Collins win. "Fine." My head whipped around, searching for someone to give me a helmet and harness. "Hey," I called to Hans who was heading toward the cabin. He turned to look at me. "Could you grab me a helmet and harness?"

He returned moments later carrying my gear. He secured the helmet on my head, noting my chattering teeth. "You okay?"

"Yup," I clipped. "Never better."

He knelt, helping me into the harness.

With my quaking knees, it was a wonder I could even get my foot through the strap.

"Just hold on tight," he said as he tightened the harness. "And know it's safe."

I scoffed, wondering how many zip lining deaths had occurred in Belgium.

The guys followed Hans and Jay, climbing to the top of the first platform. Hans hooked himself on first and took off down the line, prepared to meet everyone on the other end.

Jay hooked Cam on the line first. Cam, the daredevil in the group, howled as he took off down the line, moving faster than I could even fathom. His voice echoed throughout the vast forest spread out around us. Marcus, Z, and Trey's laughter from the platform carried down to me still at ground-level, making me even more nervous. How could they laugh at a time like this?

I dragged in an uneasy breath and made my way over to the platform they stood on. Each step shook as I willed myself to climb to the top. Marcus was being hooked to the zip line once I reached them. He stepped off the platform without a word and flew down the line, disappearing into the trees. My heart began to pound as Z was hooked on next.

He glanced to Treyton. "Catch you on the other side." He stepped off the platform and sped down the line, disappearing into the trees like Cam and Marcus had before him.

Treyton stepped up to the edge of the platform. He waved off Jay who attempted to hook him on, instead looking down at the trees below for a long time.

I wondered what he was thinking. He'd told me he wasn't a fan of heights. Was he just as terrified as me? Did he plan to back out now that he was the only band member left?

I shuffled my feet, wanting nothing more than to turn around and climb down the steps.

Trey jerked a glance over his shoulder at me, the tense lines around his eyes disappearing once he noticed me. "Ladies before gentlemen." He stepped back, leaving a direct line to the edge of the platform.

Jay gestured me over.

My body trembled. My feet felt cemented to the floor, and I couldn't move.

Trey glanced down at my feet. "Put one in front of the other."

"I know how to walk, god dammit!"

He scoffed. "So tense for someone who loves heights."

"Fuck off, Trey. Obviously, I'm terrified of them."

"See how easy it is to be honest?"

My eyes narrowed. My anger gave me guts I didn't know I possessed. I walked to the edge of the platform and looked to Jay. "Hook me up."

He did. Every click of the carabiner clips sent a jolt of nervousness through me.

Tears glazed my eyes as I turned to the zip line stretched out before me. A whoosh of air rustled the treetops beneath my feet. There was no way to go but down.

"The only way to overcome your fear is to embrace it, face it, and tell it to fuck off," Trey said from behind me.

I balked. Of all the people in the world to give me a pep talk right now, why did it have to be him? I gripped hold of the small handgrips on either side of the line, pausing for a long time.

I didn't need Trey to tell me I could do it. I *knew* I could do it. I could just lift my legs and let the line take me down. But I didn't want to. I wanted to be on solid ground at the bottom of the mountain. I didn't want to be hanging, with my life literally on the line and every part of me shaking like a leaf.

"Come on, Brie. You're one of the strongest people I know," Trey said.

I closed my eyes. Even if he was feeding me a line, it's exactly what I needed to hear in that moment. I pulled in a deep breath willing myself to step off the edge. I moved a few inches, but an invisible rope tugged me back, making me a prisoner in my own body.

"Brie. You got this," Trey said.

I shook my head, unable to turn to look at him.

"We've got the dueling lines if you want," Jay offered.

My eyes opened. "The what?"

He pointed to a line that ran parallel to my line.

With my fear overwhelming me, I hadn't even noticed it there.

"You can go on that one at the same time she goes down this one," Jay explained to Trey.

Suddenly, feeling a little hopeful, I glanced to Trey.

He said nothing as he stared at the other line.

"You're not scared, are you?" I taunted, knowing that's all it would take to get him to do it.

He looked at Jay. "Hook me up."

A lightness I hadn't felt in days emanated from my chest as Trey was hooked onto the parallel line.

"Now you both just need to step up to the edge," Jay said. "You'll never be more than three feet apart, so be careful if you extend your arms. You might hit the other."

No worries there. I had no plans to let go of the hand bar.

Trey and I both moved ourselves to the edge, lifting our hands to our bars at the same time. We glanced to each other and for the first time in a long time, I saw a softness in his gaze. Then again…it might've been fear.

"Ready?" Jay asked.

We both nodded to him before nodding to each other.

Then, taking the hugest leap of faith either of us had ever taken before, we stepped off the edge.

For a split second, I had a weightless falling sensation that told me I was plunging to my death. But the line caught me, tugging me back up. I closed my eyes and kicked up my legs. The force of my weight and the decline of the line propelled me through the air. I didn't dare let go or open my eyes as the sound of the pulley trilling down the line rivaled the sound of my pulse pounding in my ears.

"This is fucking awesome!" Trey yelled, reminding me he was still there by my side as I flew through the air faster than I'd ever moved before.

Within no time, the force of the air against my face subsided and the pulley slowed me. I came to a gradual stop, finally opening my eyes as Hans pulled me onto the platform. I looked back to the tops of the trees where we'd come from and a rush of satisfaction filled my chest. I'd done it!

"See?" Trey said as Hans helped him onto the platform. "You made it!" He threw his arms around me and held me to him.

I wanted to ignore the pride and excitement I'd seen in his eyes and just enjoy this moment of truce, but that wouldn't have been me. "Were you hoping I didn't?" I stepped out of Trey's arms, and Hans unhooked me from the first line and hooked me to the second.

Trey cocked his head. "I'm pissed at you, not a dick."

"That's debatable."

He laughed. "Seriously though. How was it?"

"Scary."

He laughed again as Hans unhooked him and hooked him to the next line. "Not exhilarating?"

"Maybe a little bit." Though I'd never admit it to him, having this experience with Trey had been necessary. No one else could've put me at as much ease as he had.

He ticked his head toward our next line. "Ready?"

I nodded, knowing I could do it.

"Bryce will meet you at the next platform," Hans told us.

We both moved to the edge of the second platform and stepped off again. This time I was a little more brazen, flying down the line with more confidence than I had the first time.

Trey howled.

I laughed.

"Try it," he called over.

"What?"

He howled again.

I howled, my voice echoing all around us.

He laughed, and when he laughed liked that, all seemed right in the world—at least for a little while.

I leaned back, trying to see how fast I could go and still feel secure. I closed my eyes and a rush of euphoria swept over me. I wanted to believe it was the rush of the zip lines. But something told me it was Trey and me coming to an understanding. Something I hadn't realized I needed until now.

CHAPTER SEVENTEEN

Brielle

"Stop there," Cam yelled from the backseat of the van on our way back to the hotel.

The driver pulled into a dirt parking lot of an old dive bar in the middle of nowhere with crooked neon signs in the windows with half the lights out.

Once the van stopped, Cam pulled open the door, and the guys piled out.

Z poked his head back in and looked to the driver. "Don't leave, man. We shouldn't be long."

The driver nodded.

"You're not coming?" Z asked me.

I shook my head.

He shrugged.

When I twisted back in my seat, I heard a tapping on the passenger window. Trey stood outside, ticking his head toward the bar.

I lowered my window. "You guys go do your thing. I crashed your party today."

He cocked his head, his blue eyes pleading with me to go inside.

Him wanting me in there, mixed with us having such a good day together, moved my hand to the door handle. He was extending an olive branch. I didn't want to ruin that. I pushed open the door and stepped out of the van.

The other guys were already crowded around the bar when we walked into the dark space.

"I ordered a pitcher," Marcus said as I slid onto a worn stool.

Cam and Z moved to the dartboard, and Marcus took off for the bathroom. Trey slipped onto the stool beside me.

"You're not playing darts?" I asked.

Trey shook his head.

"I don't need a babysitter."

He snickered. "You sure about that?"

I straightened my spine.

"Relax. I was talking about the clientele." He lowered his voice and leaned closer to me. "There are some shady characters in here."

I exhaled slowly, reminding myself to stop being so defensive and always thinking the worst about everything Trey said. "Well, like I said before, you got stuck with me today. I don't want you missing time with your friends."

"I'm not missing anything. And I didn't feel stuck."

My brows arched. "You didn't?"

He shook his head, his eyes drifting around the bar and avoiding my gaze. "Maybe I needed you today just as much as you needed me."

My stomach dipped. That was as close to a *thank you* as I'd ever received from him.

"I liked seeing you scared today," he continued, his eyes cutting back to mine. "I liked knowing big bad Brie can be vulnerable. And, despite the tough exterior, she actually needs other people. I was happy to be one of those people today."

I stared into his eyes, floored by his words.

"Nice," Marcus interrupted, squeezing between Trey and me to grab the pitcher and glasses that had been placed there. He began pouring beer into glasses, and our conversation quickly ended.

Two beers later and I'd beaten both Cam and Marcus at darts. I couldn't be sure they didn't let me win. But now I was up against Z. He would *never* let me win. He pulled back his hand and released the dart. It missed the bullseye, the only spot we both hadn't hit yet.

The guys groaned as Z grabbed the darts off the board.

"What do I get when I win?" I asked.

Z rolled his eyes, though I could see the humor behind them. "*If* you win, you get bragging rights." He held the darts out to me.

"Bragging rights? That's it?" I took the darts from him.

"Nobody ever beats Z," Cam informed me.

"Until tonight," I assured them as I threw my first dart. It hit the black eighteen slice in the top right corner of the board—nowhere near the middle.

The guys snickered.

Dammit.

I evened up my next dart, eyeing the bullseye. I released it, but it dipped, hitting the point of the three, the black slice right beneath the center.

The guys snickered again.

I evened up my last dart. I could see the bullseye.

"She'll miss," Trey whispered to the guys.

I released the dart and it hit the center of the board. My arms flew into the air, and I couldn't stop my hips from swaying from side to side in a happy dance.

Z turned to me with his hand extended. "Nice game, Superstar."

I laughed as I stilled my hips and shook his hand. Then I turned a steely gaze on Trey. "She'll miss, huh?"

I didn't let him respond, twisting and walking to the ladies' room instead.

I stepped up to the sink and washed my hands, taking in the dark circles around my eyes and my messy waves. Zip lining and drinking definitely did a number on me. I pinched my cheeks so I didn't look so pale and tried to tame my waves.

The restroom door opened then closed behind me. Once I heard the lock click, I spun around.

Trey stood against the door.

"I think you *missed* the men's room. It's next door."

He said nothing, just stared at me.

"Did you come to see if I was puking after I *didn't* miss?"

"I knew you'd make that shot."

I scoffed. "Right."

"Don't you realize that's what we do? Me and you. We push each other's buttons. We challenge each other."

I rolled my eyes. "Whatever, Trey."

He pushed off the door and stalked toward me. My ass hit the sink as I tilted my head back to meet his gaze. "I was impressed out there."

I swallowed my shock. "What?"

"None of us ever beat Z at darts, and you did. That was impressive."

I blinked, unsure how to respond.

"*And*, I was proud of you today on the zip lines too."

My eyes lowered, his words suddenly unnerving me. No one had told me they were proud of me since my mother passed away.

Trey reached up and tucked an unruly strand of hair behind my ear. "I came in here because I like dancing with you."

"What?"

His lips turned up in the corners. "They've got a jukebox out there. And I just dumped a shitload of money in it and lined up a hell of a playlist."

"Cam won't dance with you?"

"He probably would if he wasn't already on his way back to the hotel."

My brows furrowed. "He left?"

"They all did. They wanted to head back."

"And you didn't?"

He shrugged. "I wasn't ready for the day to be over yet."

A ripple rolled through my belly, his words throwing me off balance. This back and forth with him was dizzying.

"So, are you gonna dance with me or not?" he asked.

My emotions were all over the place. One minute I felt like an outsider and the next I felt included. I was struggling to keep up. "It didn't really seem like a dancing crowd out there."

"Do I look like someone who cares?"

My lips twisted as I considered his question.

Not waiting for me to make a decision, Trey stepped back and grabbed my hand. I considered resisting, but between our shared zip line experience earlier and him sticking around to hang with me, I had no reason to. I let him pull me away from the sink, out of the restroom, and into the dark bar.

An '80s hair band ballad drifted from the speakers. I glanced to him. "You chose this one?"

He laughed. "It's the best I could do in the middle of Belgium." He pulled me into the center of the floor. No one else danced, but it didn't stop him from turning toward me and wrapping his arms around me. I rested my hands on his shoulders.

This was different than dancing in the parking lot. He'd stayed behind to spend time with me, and I suddenly liked that idea way too much.

Trey stared down at me, his tongue flicking out and dragging over his bottom lip.

God. I wondered what that tongue ring would feel like in my mouth. A jolt shot between my thighs. His scent invaded my senses as the raspy sound of the singer floated through the speakers.

Trey swayed us to the music, dropping his mouth beside my ear. His breath fanned out over my neck. I held my breath, waiting for his next move. He hummed the words to the song, the vibration sending goosebumps racing up my arms.

As we moved around the empty dance floor, thoughts whirled through my head. How, after five years, had we gotten to this point? How, after the fight with Flow, were we dancing in a dive bar in Belgium?

As if he could read my thoughts, his arms tightened around me.

The final notes of the song drifted through the bar. Trey gazed down at me before inching closer. I sucked in a sharp breath. Was he going to kiss me? Did I *want* him to kiss me? Would I let him kiss me? *Should* I let him kiss me?

Clapping erupted around us.

We stilled, our eyes shifting to the people scattered around the bar who applauded our dance. Laughter burst out of Trey as I buried my head in his chest and laughed.

Another song began.

"We can't let our audience down now," Trey said as he began to move us to the music.

I lifted my head and stared up at him. A shiver rushed up my spine. I'd wanted him to kiss me. Like, right there and then, with eyes on us. Something changed today. Something inexplicable. Maybe it was a long time coming. I had no idea anymore.

The corner of his mouth lifted into a smirk, and I was beginning to think he really could hear my thoughts.

"You gonna tell me why I can't play "Clair de Lune"?" he asked.

"I was mad when I said that."

"You still mad?"

I shrugged.

He pulled me closer. "You *still* mad?"

I stifled a smile and shook my head.

"Good." He leaned down and pressed his lips to my forehead.

The intimate contact branded my skin with a tingling I hadn't felt since I was a teenager. Suddenly, I had the desire to feel his lips elsewhere and tried futilely to even my breathing that had suddenly become shaky.

Trey bent his head, his mouth hovering by my ear. "I've tried being good, Brie. I really have."

The vibration of his words sent a quiver rushing through me.

"But I can't do it anymore." He lowered his head. His breath drifting over my neck and collarbone sent my mind whirring. Then, catching me completely off guard, he licked a path from my neck to my ear.

My eyes rolled into the back of my head as the ball of his tongue ring created a dizzying sensation between the muscles in my neck. Could he feel my heart trying to escape my chest? Could he feel the electricity humming off my body?

He flicked his tongue at my earlobe, rolling the ball over the back of it.

Sweet Jesus.

"Trey," I breathed.

He said nothing, licking another path up my neck.

My knees nearly buckled as I tightened my grasp on him.

He chuckled, the devious sound rumbling against my skin. "Do you want me to stop?"

"Yes."

"Yes?" he asked, dragging his ring around the outside of my earlobe.

"No," I breathed, unable to control the throbbing between my legs.

"I haven't been able to look at you without seeing those booty shorts and belly button ring in weeks."

"Why are you so fascinated by my belly button ring?"

"Not fascinated. Turned the hell on."

I stifled a smile.

"I heard you broke up with your man."

I nodded.

He smirked, the reaction doing strange things to my belly. "You ready to get out of here?" he asked.

"Now?"

"I'd rather not start undressing you in the middle of a bar."

"Who said anything about undressing?"

He lifted an unconvinced brow.

Something about his certainty made me feel like he was seeing me as one of his groupies. Was that what I'd be if I went "home" with him? I was horny as hell, but it wasn't like we'd never see each other again. We were stuck together for the foreseeable future. Was this just a get-it-out-of-our-systems thing or did he really feel something for me? Because I honestly had no idea. One minute we were fighting, the next we were on the verge of making out like a couple of teenagers.

But I knew Trey. And for as long as I'd known him, I'd never seen him with the same girl more than once. And that wasn't me. I couldn't be that girl. "Yeah. We should head back."

"To your room or mine?" he asked with bouncing brows.

I stepped back from him and headed toward the door, trying to gather my wits about me. As much as I wanted to feel that tongue ring in other places, I needed to work with Trey. And sleeping with him, especially after I'd had a couple of drinks, seemed like a bad idea. Sleeping with him at *all*, seemed like a bad idea.

The van had returned for us and idled in the parking lot. I pulled open the front passenger door.

"Whoa," Trey said.

I glanced over my shoulder.

"You're gonna make me sit back here all alone?"

I said nothing, just climbed inside the front seat, knowing it was safer to keep a buffer between us.

A moment later, I felt the backseat dip with the weight of him as the side door slammed shut.

"Well, this sucks," he grumbled.

I swiveled in my seat to look at him. The sight of him in the backseat with dilated eyes and disheveled hair sent a surge to my chest. "You know it would only make things awkward between us."

"I'm fine with awkward."

I rolled my eyes. "I'm not those groupies. And I'm not someone who can act like nothing happened when I know it did."

"I'm not asking you to act like anything."

I cocked my head. "So, you're saying you want to be with me? Because we both know that's not you."

His eyes lowered. "I told you. I don't do anything I could get addicted to."

"Sounds like a line."

His eyes jumped to mine. "Do I need you right-fucking-now? Absolutely. Will I be the best lay you've ever had? Yup. Can I promise you a happy ending? No. I don't believe in them."

Something inside me splintered at the certainty his words held. I knew he had a rough start to life. I also knew the only people who loved him died at nearly the same time. Abandonment issues and self-preservation were to be expected. But he was a grown man. He needed to learn to let people in—people other than his bandmates—without fear of being deserted. He had to see that he forged his own future now. His choices paved the way for whatever future he wanted.

I shrugged. "I believe in happy endings. So, I'd be setting myself up for disappointment if I let this go any further."

"You're saying I'd disappoint you?"

"You just admitted you would. We want different things and have different needs."

He avoided my gaze so I took the hint, twisting back in my seat and facing the road. I wondered what the driver thought of our honest conversation because his eyes stayed on the road the entire time.

We arrived back at the hotel a little while later, and we both stepped out of the van at the same time into the dark night, walking side by side into the hotel.

"You playing tonight?" I asked, my eyes glimpsing the piano in the empty lobby.

"Probably. Got some stuff on my mind."

I didn't pry, and he didn't stop at the piano. We made our way to the bank of elevators. I pressed the button, and we both waited in uncomfortable silence. Once the doors split apart, we stepped inside. I turned to face the door, but Trey turned to face me. Once closed inside the small space, the electricity between us was palpable.

"Brie."

I wouldn't look at him. If I looked, I might not be responsible for my actions. "Yeah?"

He moved toward me. I turned for fear of him knocking me over. He moved so close that my back pressed against the side wall of the elevator. He shifted his hips and through his jeans his erection moved against me. "This is what you do to me."

"Trey."

"We could have so much fun tonight."

I huffed my frustration, especially with the word *tonight* implying it would only be one night.

"You can't tell me you haven't thought about it."

"Stop."

"You can't tell me you haven't wondered what my tongue would feel like down there."

I clenched my thighs together, having a pretty good idea of how good it would feel.

The elevator dinged, as we passed the floor beneath ours.

"Last chance," Trey said.

I dropped my eyes and shook my head. "I can't."

"Can't or won't?"

I deserved more. "Both."

The elevator dinged on our floor and the doors split apart. I hurried out, fishing in my pocket for my keycard. Trey didn't keep my pace, and the notion that he wouldn't chase me—that I wasn't worth chasing— sucked. But he *had* left the ball in my court, and I said no. I couldn't fault him for abiding by my wishes.

I reached my door and scanned my card, ducking inside before I changed my mind. I stood against the door, dragging in deep breaths. I'd never needed to say no to something I wanted so badly before. And even though I knew it was for the best, it still stung.

CHAPTER EIGHTEEN

Brielle

I brushed my teeth then slipped into the shower, needing to get Trey's scent off me. Too bad I couldn't erase the feel of his arms around me. The solidity of his erection against my stomach. The safety his presence provided.

I shampooed my hair then rinsed, ready to go to bed to sleep off the night. I turned off the water, twisted out the excess water from my hair, and wrapped a white towel around me. I walked out to the room and grabbed a tank top and shorts. I examined the shorts in my hand, wondering if Trey was lying about them turning him on.

My phone buzzed on the dresser. I grabbed it and checked the screen. My father was calling. He was the last person I needed to hear from, so I sent the call to voicemail. Once the voicemail popped up, it showed four missed voicemails from him. He must've discovered I'd terminated my working relationship with Flow. It wasn't like the firm lost him. Arthur would take good care of him.

A knock on the door had me spinning around.

Oh, God. Please don't tell me he flew here.

I went to the door, scared by what I might find on the other side. I inched toward the peephole and looked through it. I sucked in a sharp breath.

Trey stood outside my room, his hands in the pockets of his basketball shorts and his eyes cast down.

"What is it, Trey?" I called through the door.

"I need to talk to you."

"I just got out of the shower. I'm not dressed."

His eyes flashed up. He stared at the peephole, essentially right at me. "Open the door, Brie."

"No."

"Brie. I'm gonna need you to open the door."

The intensity in his eyes and the butterflies swarming in my belly were too much. I reached for the deadbolt, still not sure if I should let him in. I unlocked it then grasped the door handle. I pulled in a breath then tugged the door open.

Trey stepped forward, forcing me to backpedal into the room. He slammed the door shut with his foot and grasped my cheeks between his hands. My heart slammed against the wall of my chest as I stared up into his eyes.

"I lied," he said.

"About what?"

"I told you I stayed away from things I could get addicted to."

I tilted my head, confused.

"But I can't stay away from you."

My eyebrows shot up, all coherent thoughts escaping me.

"I know I screw up and give you grief. And I know we can't seem to get along for more than a few days at a time. But there's something about you, Brie. Something that challenges me. Something that makes me want to fight with *you* more than anyone else on this planet. Because when you finally come around and smile at me, like really smile and mean it, I'm a goner."

I swallowed hard, not knowing what to say. I wanted him there. I wanted him saying more of these things to me. I wanted to keep feeling the way I did in that moment. "Stay."

Relief washed over his features. "Thank God." He lowered his face toward mine. "You won't regret this."

God, I hoped he was right.

He closed the distance between us, but instead of kissing me, he dragged the ball of his tongue ring along the seam of my lips. My legs quivered as tingles parted my lips. I wrapped my arms around his neck as our lips collided. His tongue dove inside my mouth, tangling with mine in a frantic race. The tongue ring was a welcome intrusion, stroking away at my tongue with delicious swipes. Then he shifted it to the roof of my mouth. *Holy hell.* The numbing sensations sent my eyes pinching tight. I chased the rush, keeping pace with his lips and melting into his body.

His hands dropped to my hips and he walked me back toward the bed. The backs of my legs touched it and he lowered me onto the soft white comforter, following me down. His fingers tunneled through my wet hair as his tongue continued tousling with mine. His hips shifted and his erection pressed between my legs against the towel. *Good Lord.*

His mouth pulled away from mine. We stared at each other for what seemed like forever, our chests heaving in tandem. His lips pulled into a smirk before he lowered them to my neck, lavishing me with open-mouth kisses there. "God, you taste so good."

Goosebumps erupted over my bare skin.

He kissed his way down to my shoulder. "I can't wait to know if you taste like this everywhere."

My clit began to throb as visions of his face between my legs clouded my mind.

My fingertips trailed up his back and into his hair as he kissed across the exposed area of my chest above the towel.

"For someone who always has the last word," he said between kisses, "You're pretty quiet."

"Stop talking," I groaned.

He chuckled against my skin before sitting on his knees, reaching behind his neck, and pulling his T-shirt over his head. I tried not to gawk, but he was built like an athlete, tatted up like the rock star he was, and *so* freaking hot.

And while seeing him shirtless on stage may have been one thing, having him on top of me with his shirt off and his erection pressed against me was something else entirely. He stared into my eyes without saying a word. And even with the towel on me, I felt exposed and vulnerable under his gaze. We were in uncharted territory. And I was terrified.

"I wish you could see you the way I do," he said, covering me with his body. His mouth recaptured mine. He knew how to kiss. He knew how to make me feel sexy. He knew how to turn me on like no one else before him.

My hands slipped down his back, gliding over the muscular ridges as my fingers made their way down to his basketball shorts. If I thought about all the reasons it was a bad idea, I'd stop. So, I didn't. My fingers slipped beneath the elastic waistband and my hands drifted over his ass.

He pulled out of the kiss, undoubtedly observing my labored breaths and flushed cheeks. "Let me help you." He reached down and pushed his shorts to his feet, kicking them the rest of the way off.

This was getting real. This was getting really freaking real.

Knowing my nerves would fail me if I didn't act quickly, I reached for the top of my towel where I'd tucked it in place.

Trey watched me, his eyes fixed on my fingers. "You sure?"

"No."

He quirked a brow.

"But it's happening anyway."

His lips slipped into a cocky smirk. "Damn right it is."

My eyes shifted away, almost embarrassed to be giving in. But there was no way, physically or emotionally, that I wouldn't allow myself to live in this moment. I was single, turned on, and completely enraptured by this guy I'd known for five years who I was just beginning to understand.

He rolled off of me, laying on his side beside me. "May I?" he asked, reaching for my hands on the top of my towel and covering them with his own hands.

My heart raced faster—if that was even possible. My nerves began to falter. But I steeled them and untucked the top of the towel with Trey's assistance. Had his hands not been there, I probably would've stopped. But he slowly unwrapped my towel, leaving us both naked.

Though I knew he wanted to check me out, his eyes stayed on mine. Catching me completely off guard, he lifted his hand to my cheek and his thumb drifted gently over my skin. "I wasn't lying, Brie. You've done something to me."

My eyes dropped to his erection. "I'd say."

He chuckled, and it somehow alleviated the anxiety I was feeling in that moment.

Feeling bold, I reached down and grasped hold of him. He sucked in a breath. He was big—much bigger than Keith—and I was mesmerized. I pumped my hand slowly, feeling confident with him in my grasp.

He hissed. "Fuck, Brie."

His pleasure urged me on.

He allowed me a couple more minutes. Then, he rolled on top of me and pinned my arms at my sides. "That is not how I plan to come tonight." For the first time, his eyes dropped to my breasts. He lowered his mouth and took a nipple between his lips, flicking the ball of his tongue ring against it.

My head dropped back, pushing into the pillow as my breathing released in short quick tandems like the beating of my heart. This silent torture was like nothing I'd ever felt before. Pure euphoria swept over me with each swipe of his tongue. "*Mmmmm*," I breathed.

He switched sides, using his tongue ring to flick and swirl around my other nipple. My eyes rolled into the back of my head before pinching shut. A slow swirling sensation built between my legs. My clit throbbed, intensifying each time the ring caught my nipple, sending zingers rocking through me. My legs began to tremble.

Trey continued his assault as his right hand released my arm and drifted down my hip. His calloused fingers coasted over the smooth skin of my belly. I knew what he had planned before he did it. His thumb circled my belly button then slid lightly over my belly button ring.

His hand continued down, reaching between my legs. I sucked in a breath as he slipped two fingers inside of me. My back arched off the bed as he pumped his fingers. Spiraling began between my thighs. He added his thumb to my clit and the coiling tightened, releasing in a wave of tremors out to every part of my body. Trey continued sucking my nipples, carrying me through my orgasm and milking my body of all he could.

When I came down from the mother of all orgasms, he released my nipple with a pop and pulled back, staring at what could only be described as my content face. "I could watch you come all night long."

"That better mean you intend to do *that* all night long."

He chuckled. "Oh, I've got other plans for us."

I wished his promise didn't make me long for a lot more—and not just in this hotel room. "Yeah?"

He lowered his head and kissed me hard. Then, pulled back. "Hold on." He rolled off me and grabbed for his shorts on the floor. He returned with a condom. I watched as he rolled it on. He hadn't lied when he said he protected himself, and I appreciated him being prepared.

He looked back to me to find my eyes mesmerized by his naked body. He grabbed hold of his erection and slowly pumped his hand knowing I was watching.

What. A. Turn. On.

That spiraling between my legs started again.

"You ready for me?" he asked as he continued pumping his fist.

I nodded, needing him inside of me.

He climbed over me again and positioned himself between my legs. I opened wider, giving him easier access. He rolled his hips and I held my breath, anticipating his size. He prodded me gently with the tip before pushing the rest of the way inside.

The back of my head pushed into the pillow and my back arched as I took all of him in. He stared down at me as he thrust into me at a leisurely pace. "You feel so damn good," he said.

"I won't last if you do that all night long."

He lifted a brow. "Oh, no?"

I slipped my hands around his hips and down to his ass, feeling his cheeks tighten with every thrust. He kept the same pace, but I needed him deeper. I dug my fingernails into his ass cheeks.

He didn't take the hint.

"Harder," I urged.

"Fuck, Brie. I love hearing you talk like that." His thrusts became faster and deeper, stretching me wide. He dropped his mouth to my neck and sucked on my skin.

I didn't care if he left a mark because the sensations bubbling between my legs overpowered every conceivable thought in my head. All my focus was on that spot between my legs. Like a volcano erupting, the bubbling became quicker and more intense.

"Jesus, Brie. I'm not gonna be able to hold off much longer," he said through clenched teeth.

I lifted my knees up high. He linked his arms beneath them, holding them up as he drove into me, harder and faster. "Oh, God," I said as my body once again betrayed me sending a rush of tremors racing through me.

"*Grrrr.*" Trey stilled inside me. His ragged breathing and lack of coherent words were a heady concoction.

I kissed his chest as he came down from what seemed to be a hell of an orgasm.

He slowly lifted his head and met my gaze. "What the hell have we been waiting for?"

CHAPTER NINETEEN

Treyton

I glanced down at the long dark hair spread out over my chest. The rays of sunlight sneaking through the hotel curtains cast a soft glow on Brie's hair, enabling me to see the lighter hues of brown in her hair.

I guess this was what waking up next to someone feels like.

I fought the urge to run my fingers through her pretty curls. Instead, I savored the scent drifting from them. I needed to play this right. I couldn't sneak out. Then she'd think she was just some one-night stand. But I'd never done this morning-after thing before. If she woke, I was at a loss. I didn't want to fuck it up already, but this was uncharted territory for me.

"If you try to sneak out, I will kill you," Brie's raspy morning voice warned.

"Oh yeah?" I chuckled. "How?"

"Slowly. And painfully."

I smiled, rolling her onto her back so I could see her face. Her eyes were opened just a crack as she squinted up at me.

"You're pretty in the morning," I said.

"How many girls have you said that to before?"

"Just you."

"*Right.*"

I chuckled. "Seriously, Brie. You gotta know I'm not the type of guy who sticks around until the morning."

She said nothing.

"What are you thinking?" I asked, uneasy about where her mind may have drifted. Was she thinking about all the girls she assumed I'd been with?

She shrugged.

"Tell me," I urged, more for my own peace of mind than anything else.

"I'm scared."

I sighed. "Yeah."

"So, you agree that this could be really bad?" she asked.

"Or really good," I countered.

A small smile tipped her lips.

"Because if last night was any indication, it could be fucking amazing."

She turned her head, trying to bury her face in the pillow. "Stop."

"I'm serious. That thing you did with your hand—"

"Stop it, Trey."

"Why?"

"You're embarrassing me."

Brie was embarrassed? That's something I never thought I'd see. "You weren't embarrassed last night."

She growled, and it was so damn cute.

"Was it because you realized how good we were together?"

She peeked up at me, her dubious green eyes narrowed. "How's this ever going to work?"

I shrugged. "We'll figure it out."

She cocked her head, uncertainty heavy in her eyes.

"It looks like you're doubting me."

She said nothing.

"Well, let me show you what happens when you doubt me." I inched down her body, running my nose between her breasts. I continued my descent, breathing in her fresh scent, before burying my face between her legs.

"Trey," she gasped as my tongue licked a path up her seam, flicking her clit with the ball of my tongue ring. "*Gahhhhh,*" she moaned.

"Believe me yet?" I asked.

She paused. "No."

That little vixen. She *wanted* me to torture her. And I fucking loved that she did. I flicked her clit again. Her back arched, her breasts lifted, and her hips shifted so she was closer to my face. I assaulted her clit, using my tongue ring to drive her wild. Who was I kidding? Tasting her was driving me wild.

"Trey," she said, all breathy and turned on.

I continued my torture, knowing the tongue ring worked magic like nothing else.

She began to pant, her body quaked, and her knees closed tightly around my head. It didn't deter me. I kept licking her until she writhed, her pleasure obviously becoming unbearable. I finally relented as her ragged breathing subsided and her knees relaxed. I climbed back up her body and covered her with mine. I planted kisses all over her satiated face, knowing she'd never let me kiss her mouth with her juices on my tongue. She wrapped her arms around me and held me where I lay.

"*Now*, what are you thinking?" I said.

"Same thing you were last night. Why'd we wait so long?"

"Truth?" I asked her.

She nodded.

"Because you finally dropped the bitch mask."

She scoffed.

I rolled off her, turning on my side and resting my cheek in my palm. "I'm serious, Brie. Why the hell did you have to be so tough?"

She pulled the comforter over her body and I let her—for the time being. "It's what I saw my father do. It's how he got respect from his clients. He was no-nonsense, direct, and detached."

"But that's not you, Brie. I can see that now."

She shrugged. "It kept people at arm's length, separated my job from my personal life, and protected me from temptations like you."

"Temptation, huh?"

"Uh, *yeah.*"

I laughed, loving her honesty. "You owe me another fact."

She groaned. "I just gave you one."

"Yeah, but we skipped a few days."

"Whose fault was that?" she sassed.

I ignored her question and asked my own. "How long do you think you'll work for the band?"

Her eyes grew wide. "Why? Do you not like me working for you guys?"

"What? No." *Great, I was already fucking things up.* "I was just curious if you'll eventually move on."

She paused for a long time. I worried I'd pissed her off. "Can you promise not to say anything to anyone?" she finally said.

I nodded, intrigued.

"I want to take over Artists Limited when my father retires—if he lets me."

"Is there a chance he won't? You're his daughter."

She rolled her eyes. "I didn't have the childhood people probably assume I had. And he and I don't have the father-daughter relationship people might assume we do."

"People say he's a real dick."

"You don't know the half."

"Then tell me," I urged, wanting to know more about her.

She shook her head. "What *you* went through as a kid was a hundred times worse than me."

I reached over and grasped her chin so she had no choice but to look me in the eyes. "Everyone deals with shit, Brie. It's not something to compare. If it happened to you, it still matters."

"Yeah, well, let's just say, he pretty much deserted me once my mom died."

"I didn't know you lost your mom. When?"

She paused, chewing nervously on her bottom lip. "When I was ten."

My heart clenched in my chest. I'd lost my parents when *I* was ten.

She nodded, knowing I grasped the similarity between us. "'Clair de Lune' was her favorite song. She used to play it on the piano for me," she explained.

Son of a bitch. "I'm sorry, Brie. I should've stopped the second you asked me to."

She shrugged.

"My mom loved when I played it for *her*," I admitted.

Brie's mouth parted, grasping why I hadn't wanted to stop.

"It sucks losing a parent so young," I said, now knowing we'd both endured the same heartache of losing a mother.

Brie nodded. "And you lost two."

"So, did you. Even if one of them was still living."

"I don't think he ever wanted to be a father," she explained. "It wasn't like he ever lived with my mom and me anyway. He was a selfish bastard staying in the city while we were home. Who knew what he was doing? My mom dying was probably a blessing for him. He had a nanny raise me until I left for college."

I couldn't hide the disgust in my voice. "Why the hell are you working for him?"

"You're just gonna think I'm screwed up," she said.

I shook my head. "No, I won't."

Time seemed to stall, and I wondered if me grilling her was making her angry. "I needed him to see what he had and what he missed out on. I'm an amazing person, and he has no idea because he's never tried to get to know me. It's why I want his company. I want to make it a hundred times better than it is right now. And I want to prove what I'm truly capable of doing without him there."

I said nothing. Brie never seemed like someone who had anything to prove to anyone. She'd always been headstrong and confident. But now I could see that she was just as vulnerable as everyone else. She just wanted to be loved by a father who seemed incapable of showing her love. "Go get showered and meet me downstairs in half an hour."

Her brows lifted, likely surprised by my subject change.

"I wanna take you to get something to eat," I explained.

I'd like to believe the excitement in her eyes was due to my breakfast offer, but now knowing what I knew about her, I think she'd needed the assurance that this hadn't just been a one-night stand. "I want waffles," she said.

"Waffles?"

"We're in Belgium. We need Belgian waffles."

I smiled, unexpectedly eager to get her some waffles. "Of course we do."

She reached off the side of the bed and grabbed my shirt that I'd tossed on the nightstand.

"What are you doing?"

"Covering up."

"Why? I've seen and tasted most of you."

Again, she turned her head, trying to bury her face in the pillow.

I grasped her chin again and turned her to look me in the eyes. "I love how you look. Don't you dare try to hide from me."

She rolled her eyes.

"Stop doubting me," I warned her.

She tucked her lips, though I could almost hear her begging for the kind of torture I was so talented at giving.

"I'm gonna head back to my room and clean up," I said. "Then I'll take you to get your waffles."

She smiled, and it was as if I was seeing her for the very first time. I'd never noticed the sparkle in her eyes when she was excited before—likely because I'd never given her a reason to be excited. Now, it was all I could think about doing.

I snatched my shirt from her hand and pulled it over my head, before grabbing my shorts from the floor and tugging them on under Brie's close appraisal. "Like what you see?"

She nodded.

I chuckled. "See you in thirty minutes. Don't be late."

"Or what?"

I laughed again as I walked out of the room, wondering what else I could do to keep that smile on Brie's face.

Brielle

The door clicked as Trey stepped out of my room. I rolled over, tightening the comforter around me and burying my face in the pillow. *Oh, my freaking God.* I needed to shower, but my body was physically spent and my brain whirled with questions. What had we just done?

Last night had been amazing. Like nothing I'd ever experienced before. I crawled off the bed and made my way into the shower, letting the water bring my body back to Earth. I hated washing Trey's scent off of me but knowing I'd be with him again shortly made it easier. I hopped out of the shower and dried my hair, opting to leave it down. I dressed in skinny jeans, a hoodie, and Chucks and slipped out of the room with a couple of minutes to spare.

I arrived in the lobby to find Trey sitting on a sofa with Cam. Disappointment filled me. Had he invited Cam? Was this not the romantic day I'd envisioned when he asked to take me out? Was he trying to keep it platonic and I hadn't gotten the memo?

Trey stood when he saw me approach, a smooth smirk slipping across his lips as his eyes assessed me slow and purposefully. "Hey."

Cam twisted to see who'd stolen his attention. "'Sup, Brielle?"

"Hey." I looked to Trey, not knowing what was happening.

"You ready?" he asked me.

I nodded.

"Later, Cam."

Cam jumped up. "Where ya going?"

"Grabbing some breakfast," Trey said.

"Just the two of you?" he asked, disbelief coloring his tone.

"Yup," Trey said before turning away from him and leading me out the front door.

Fans must not have known the band was staying there since no one was outside the hotel. We hopped into a waiting van, and it drove us through the quaint little town where we were staying.

"Glad you decided to sit next to me this time," Trey said as he dropped his arm over the back of my shoulders in the backseat.

I rolled my eyes. He knew full well why I couldn't sit next to him the previous night.

His eyes assessed my casual outfit. "You look nice."

I laughed. "I look nice?"

"You always look nice."

My eyes drifted over his jeans and black T-shirt.

"You don't have to say it," he said. "I know I always look good."

I bumped him with my shoulder. "Don't make me rethink this."

"Rethink what?" he asked, his brows raised in question.

Though it wasn't at all what I'd been talking about, I said, "Breakfast."

He grunted, and I wondered if he'd been trying to get me to admit what I considered us.

The van stopped on a brick road lined with little stores and cafés, all with their own personality. Trey handed the driver some cash and we stepped out. We looked around, wondering which way to go. It didn't take long to spot someone walking down the street with a waffle piled high with whipped cream.

Catching me off guard, Trey grabbed my hand and led me to a small window service shop with a glass showcase in front filled with waffles with different toppings.

"I want chocolate," I said, eyeing the one with whipped cream covered in zig-zagged chocolate syrup.

"For breakfast?"

"Any time of the day," I assured him.

He laughed and pointed to one topped with strawberries and whipped cream. "I'm having that one."

We ordered and the man behind the counter passed them over to us. I reached for my money.

"Don't," Trey said, handing his money to the man.

"Thank you," I said.

"Don't thank me. I plan to eat half of yours."

I turned away from him with my paper plate, guarding my food. "Who said I'm sharing?"

"I did."

We took our plates and forks and walked down the narrow street packed with people. I dug into my waffle and took a bite, savoring the chocolaty goodness with a quiet moan.

Trey bit into his. "*Mmmmmmmm.*"

We smiled with our mouths filled, knowing these were the best waffles either of us had ever tasted.

"Amazing, right?" I said.

He nodded. "Try mine." He took a bite and held it between his teeth. Instead of chewing it, he leaned over and kissed me, his un-chewed piece of waffle ending up in my mouth.

I pulled back and chewed the fruity piece of waffle. Then, nodded my approval.

Trey leaned back in and kissed me right. His lips moving fervently with mine. When he pulled away, our breathing was labored. "I didn't think kissing you could be as good in the sunlight," he said.

"Why?"

"Because it was damn good in the dark."

I laughed.

"I like kissing you, Brie. Way too much."

I took a bite of my waffle, needing to stifle the smile that fought to take over my entire face.

"That's not fair," he said.

"What?"

"I shared with you."

I used my fork to tear off another piece of my waffle. I held it out to him. He shook his head. I cocked my head, knowing what he was requesting. And while it was sexy as hell when he did it, I didn't hold the same sexiness factor as him.

"I'm waiting," he urged.

I rolled my eyes before popping the piece into my mouth and kissing Trey. He took over, swiping it off my tongue. A huge grin spread across his face as he chewed it. "You were right. Chocolate is good any time of the day."

"When are you gonna learn? I'm right about most things."

"Most things?" he said. "What have you been wrong about?"

"Oh, I don't know. A certain drummer."

Trey laughed, the sound working its way into every little cracked crevice in my body.

We finished our waffles and tossed our dishes in a trash receptacle on the side of the street.

A woman and little girl with pigtails nabbed my attention. They stood in front of a book shop staring at us. I could tell the mom was a fan by the way her eyes were locked on Trey and her smile stretched across her face.

"I think you've been spotted," I said to Trey.

He twisted around, spotting the woman.

A flush spread across her cheeks.

Girl, I know the feeling.

Trey waved, and she held up her phone—the universal "can I get a photo" motion. Trey approached the pair, crouching in front of the little girl first. "Hey there, little lady. Are you a Savage Beasts' fan?"

She shook her head.

"Ouch." He grabbed his heart, pretending to be wounded by her honest answer.

"But my mommy is," she said.

His brows shot up. "Oh, yeah?" He lowered his voice to a whisper. "You think she'll take a picture with me?"

The little girl nodded.

"You wanna be in the picture, too?" he asked.

She nodded again, this time grinning and revealing a missing front tooth.

Between the adorable little girl and Trey's interaction with her, I didn't want the whole scene to end. But I knew the woman was eager to get a photo with Trey, so I approached her. "Would you like me to take the picture for you?"

"Yes." She handed me her phone. "Thank you so much."

Trey stood up and greeted her. "I hope *you're* the fan."

The woman laughed. "Yes. Absolutely."

Trey wrapped his arms around her, hugging her like she was someone he'd known for years. "What's your name?"

"Idella," she whispered, likely awed by the feel of his arms and amazing scent.

"Good to meet you, Idella." Trey stepped back. "Brie, you taking our picture?"

I held up the phone.

Trey scooped up the little girl in one arm and wrapped his arm around Idella.

I snapped a bunch of pictures as the three of them smiled. I handed Idella back her phone, and Trey spent a few more minutes speaking to her before saying goodbye.

"You were adorable with that little girl," I said as we continued making our way down the street.

"Yeah?"

"It was hot."

His brows shot up. "Yeah?" He grabbed my shoulders and backed me against the side of a shop, inching toward me and caging me in with his body. "I'm having a hard time keeping my mouth off yours." Our lips collided and a rush of elation swept over my body as the taste of chocolate and strawberry mixed.

"*Prenez une chambre*," an old woman mumbled as she passed by us.

Trey pulled out of the kiss. "Oh, I just gotta know what that meant." He slipped his phone out and repeated her words into a translation app.

"Get a room," his phone said.

I burst out laughing.

"Oh, believe me," Trey called after her. "I plan to make good use of that room."

I shook my head, amused and embarrassed. But happy. Way too happy.

CHAPTER TWENTY

Brielle

BJ and I arrived at the indoor venue before the guys arrived. I met with the VIP and fan club members who anxiously waited to meet the band and prepared them for what to do when the band arrived. As soon as I heard chatter from the arena's back door, I knew the guys had entered the building. An unfamiliar anxiousness filled me. I hadn't realized how eager I was to see Trey after our morning together.

The guys filed into the room and took their places by the venue's backdrop.

"How many tonight?" Z asked me.

"About fifty," I said, avoiding Trey's eyes which I could feel were on me.

I needed to do my job like I always had. Letting on that anything was going on between Trey and me was the least professional thing I could've done.

"I'm gonna go get them." I turned to the door and pulled it open. I motioned in the first two fans. "Ready?"

The girls' heads bobbed and they hurried inside. Their short denim skirts barely covered their asses and their crop tops might as well have been bras. They threw their arms around each of the guys as they greeted them, making sure to reach down and grab their asses.

Inwardly, I rolled my eyes. Some girls had no shame.

I glanced to Trey and lifted my brows to let him know I'd seen the girls' antics. He winked at me, then ran his tongue ring along his bottom lip.

My core tingled as recollections of the things he'd done to me with that tongue flashed through my mind.

"Can you take the picture?" one of the girls asked me, snapping me out of my sexy daydream.

"Of course," I said, taking her phone as she and her friend squeezed in between the guys. "Everyone smile."

They all did, even Trey this time.

Once the girls said goodbye, I led the next pair into the room. They were gorgeous and as much as I hated to admit it, my eyes instantly shot to Trey's.

It was as if he'd known I'd watch his reaction because his eyes were locked on mine instead.

"Nicely played," I mouthed to him.

He shrugged, and, for the first time, I knew what it felt like to be Aubrey. I understood her staying away from the meet and greet area. These female fans wanted their moment to touch and be in the arms of their favorite rock stars. We were the girls who got to be with them when all the fanfare died down—when the guys were at their most vulnerable and most real. These girls got the rock star fantasy for a couple of minutes. What *we* got was so much more.

Removing ourselves was the perfect solution. But I worked for them. It was my job to take care of this part of the tour while on the road with the band. I couldn't mess it up by getting jealous or possessive.

But I wouldn't lie and say it was easy.

The meet and greet eventually ended, and the guys were hurried backstage and right onto the stage. Apparently, the Belgium crowd did not like to be kept waiting. And Savage Beasts never disappointed their fans.

I watched from the side of the stage. The band blew it out of the park with their set, each song better than the last. I watched Trey pound away at his drums, the sticks an extension of his arms. He said he couldn't keep his lips off me. Well, I couldn't keep my eyes off him. He was born to be a musician. The music, no matter which instrument he played, just flowed from his body.

"How was breakfast?" Aubrey asked.

I looked over my shoulder at her standing there. "Huh?"

"Oh, don't even. Cam said you and Treyton took off together and didn't invite him."

I tried not to smile but I couldn't contain it.

Aubrey's eyes widened. "I knew it."

I paused, considering all the reasons it was a bad idea to tell anyone—especially Z's fiancé, but I was so damn happy. I couldn't hide it. "Do the others know?"

She shook her head. "They're all oblivious. Even Cam who spilled the news. They all just thought you were trying to bury the hatchet."

I nodded, knowing that was a likely story.

"But that's not what you were doing, was it?" she pried.

"We're figuring things out."

She smiled. "That makes me so happy. I like Treyton. And I like you. You both deserve to be as happy as me and Kozart."

"We're not exactly at that point yet," I said.

"And we didn't start there either."

She had a point. And honestly, I was just happy to be figuring anything out with Trey.

A short while later, the crowd roared as the guys finished their set. I moved away from the side of the stage and gathered my belongings backstage.

My heart began to race. Would Trey ignore me or greet me the way Z always did Aubrey? The guys filed backstage, Z beelining it to Aubrey while Trey, Cam, and Marcus grabbed food and drinks.

A pit formed in my stomach, and the fact that it did pissed me off. I didn't want anyone to suspect anything was going on between Trey and me, but at the same time, the stupid girl in me wanted him to stake his claim on me for all to see.

"Hey, Brie," Trey called.

I pulled in a sharp breath, then turned to find him by the food table.

"You want something to eat?"

My eyes widened. Was he talking about food or him? My eyes jumped nervously around, but no one paid him or me any attention, except Aubrey who smirked. "I'm fine," I assured him.

He smirked. "Yes, you are."

Again, my eyes flashed around. They locked on Cam's. His narrowed, as if he couldn't figure out why Trey was acting so odd.

I spotted BJ by the door and hurried over to him. "What time are we heading out?" Our next stop was France which I couldn't wait to visit, especially if it meant spending time there with Trey.

"Soon."

"I'm gonna head onto the bus. Get cleaned up before you get on," I said.

He nodded.

I glanced back, hoping to catch Trey's eyes to say goodbye, but he was in the middle of an animated discussion with Marcus. I'd text him later.

I left the building and stepped onto the bus, ready for the overnight trip to France. I brushed my teeth and changed into black shorts and a pink tank top. I tried to keep covered up while BJ and I shared a space. He'd given me the back bedroom for this leg of the trip, but we'd been good about switching every other country. Because no matter how cozy they tried to make them, those aisle bunk beds were uncomfortable.

I grabbed my phone and slipped under the comforter, wanting to keep my mind off a certain drummer who was consuming my every thought. Two more missed calls from my father appeared on my screen. He hadn't left voicemails. Good thing. I hadn't listened to any of the others anyway. This distance from him had been good. Him being able to barge into my office and make demands of me whenever he saw fit wasn't healthy. Being able to ignore his calls had been therapeutic. I dismissed the calls and opened the book I'd been reading.

A chapter into it, I heard the bus door slide open and footsteps move toward my room. BJ knew when the door was closed to respect my privacy. But he knocked on my door.

I sat up. "What's up?"

He said nothing.

"BJ?"

The door handle turned and the door pushed open. Trey stood there in low hanging basketball shorts and a sleeveless navy T-shirt. His eyes assessed me sitting in bed. "You're all ready for me, I see."

"What are you doing here?"

He stepped inside my small space and closed the door behind him. "I wanted to see you. And I have something for you." He reached into his pocket and pulled out a bag of M&M's.

My eyes rounded as he handed them to me. "How'd you know?"

He sat down on the edge of the bed. "I pay attention."

"Thank you." I tore into the bag and poured a handful into my hand, picking out some of the red and yellow ones and popping them into my mouth.

Trey held out his hand and I poured some into his palm.

"My mom always ate them," I explained. "She said nothing could be wrong if you had chocolate."

"That explains your love of chocolate at any hour."

I laughed. "Where's BJ?"

"With the guys."

The bus lurched.

"Wait. He's riding to France with the guys?"

Trey nodded. "You okay with that?"

"Of course. But what did you tell them?"

He shrugged. "Just said we had unfinished business. No one questioned that."

"*Do* we have unfinished business?"

He lifted his hand and traced the pad of his thumb along my bottom lip. "Yup."

Ripples rolled through my belly. "So, you're staying with me all night?"

"All night long," he assured me. "What shall we do?"

I chuckled, having a few ideas of my own.

He leaned forward and pressed his lips to mine, sending tingles spreading down to my toes. He pulled back and stared at me. "You looked jealous at the meet and greet."

"For the last time, I don't get jealous."

"Bullshit."

"Nope."

"So, you're saying, if I let those girls put their hands all over me, kiss me even, you wouldn't be upset."

"Do you want me to be jealous?" I asked.

"I want you to be naked."

I laughed. That was Trey. Never serious for very long. That was one of his most endearing qualities. "You first."

He howled his delight as he stood from the bed and began to tug off his shirt.

"Wait."

He stopped, his eyes narrowed.

I climbed out from under the comforter and stepped in front of him. "Let me do it."

"By all means." He dropped his hands to his sides.

Over his T-shirt, I pressed my hands to his chest. His eyes dropped to my hands as they drifted slowly down his chest, reveling in the feel of him beneath the fabric. His muscles underneath were as solid as they looked on stage as he pounded away at the drums. I stopped at the hem of his shirt, dipping my fingertips underneath and tugging it up. He lifted his arms so the shirt slipped effortlessly over his head and off his arms. His eyes followed my hand as I tossed it aside.

My hands returned to his shoulders, slowly drifting down his biceps and tracing the intricate tattoos on his left arm with my fingertips. From the music notes to the drumsticks over the piano keys and around the wings of the eagles, my fingertips explored them all.

I shamelessly breathed in his just-showered scent as my fingers drifted back to his bare chest, coasted down his torso, and dipped into every ridge of his washboard abs.

"Enjoying yourself?" he asked.

I nodded as my fingers stopped on the waist of his shorts.

"What's your next move?"

My fingertips slipped under the elastic waistband.

He sucked in a sharp breath.

God, I loved that sound. I grabbed hold of the waist and tugged the shorts down his legs. He stepped out of them, leaving them on the floor.

I stared at him standing naked in front of me, drinking in every inch of his body.

"Now what?"

"I hadn't thought that far ahead."

His low chuckle sent crazy vibrations through my nerve endings. "Then I think it's my turn." Trey grasped hold of my shoulders and turned me away from him. His chest pressed to my back as his lips settled beneath my right ear sending shivers down my spine. He peppered my neck and collarbone with open-mouth kisses as his big calloused drummer hands slipped under my tank top. His thumb circled my belly button ring before his fingertips traveled across my stomach.

His hands drifted up slowly, cupping my breasts. He pinched my nipples, sending a powerful jolt between my thighs. My breathing became labored, the sensations weakening my knees. He released my nipples and dragged his thumbs around them in mind-blowing circles, the path of his thumbs mimicking his tongue ring's movement the previous night. The mere thought, mixed with his fingers on me, brought on waves of pleasure.

"Take off your shorts," he said.

He didn't release my breasts, continuing his glorious torture as I pushed down my shorts.

"Hold on a sec," he said. Only then did he release me to grab a foil packet from his shorts on the floor. I didn't move as I heard the tear of the packet cut through the quiet space. I could feel him roll on the condom behind me before his hands grasped the hem of my tank top and pulled it up and off me. His hands returned to my breasts, pinching my nipples for good measure. I gasped.

He turned us so he could sit on the bed, pulling me down gently so I straddled him. "Sit down on me."

I shifted my ass until I felt his erection pressing against me. Nope. Not that hole. I shifted again until I easily sank down to the hilt on his lap, taking him all in.

We'd never been face to face like this. Never this close—this exposed. And I liked it. I rocked my hips, moving back and forth slowly.

He leaned forward and kissed me hard, his tongue pushing inside my mouth for a long breathtaking kiss. He pulled away, burying his mouth in the crook of my neck and assaulting my skin with open-mouth kisses that made my eyes cross. He reached up and his fingers rolled my nipples in a steady torture.

I moved faster, back and forth, finding my rhythm.

"God. Just like that," he said.

I tried sinking deeper as I moved my hips. I loved being in control. Loved controlling his pleasure. His hands moved up and he cupped my cheeks, yanking my mouth back to his. His tongue pushed back inside and tangled with mine as both of us jockeyed for control— the irony of our entire relationship not lost on me.

Needing to catch his breath, Trey eventually pulled back. He gazed into my eyes as we both gasped for air. "Crawl onto the bed."

I didn't question it. I lifted my hips and Trey pulled out of me. I crawled onto the bed on all fours facing away from him, anxious for whatever he had in mind.

He stood from the bed, seemingly standing behind me and not joining me on the bed. I held my breath, listening for his next move. He grabbed hold of my hips and pulled my ass to the edge of the bed. I felt the heat of his body move behind me, and he thrust into me from behind.

My back arched as my hands fought to keep me steady. His thrusts were powerful. My fingers clawed at the comforter, holding on for support as he thrust in and out of me. My knees began to tremble as he hit my g-spot over and over again from that angle. My eyes squeezed shut as I tried to prolong it. But I was close. Very close. Given Trey's grunts, he was too. A stir of tingles began between my legs, and I couldn't hold off any longer. One more thrust and a wave of tremors shot through my body, numbing every one of my nerve endings. Trey continued thrusting into me faster and harder. It didn't take long. He released a long satisfied growl and stilled inside me. Neither of us said a word. There was no reason. Trey lowered me down to the bed and covered my back with his sweaty body, breathing heavy behind me.

This was our second night together—a record in Trey's life. And that alone spoke volumes.

CHAPTER TWENTY-ONE

Brielle

I awoke sprawled across Trey's chest, savoring the feel of his body beneath mine. The soft purr of his breathing, mixed with the bus tires moving over the concrete highway, was such a soothing sound. I hoped the fact that he'd slept through the night for the second time with me without having to find a piano meant he was content. And I really hoped I had something to do with it.

The purring disappeared and Trey shifted slightly. "Why are you up?" his raspy voice whispered.

"Just thinking."

"About what?" he asked, wrapping his arms around me and holding me against him. "Tell me it involves your mouth on my body."

"Maybe a little."

He chuckled.

"No, I was just thinking about all the places I want to visit. I've never been to France."

"I've never been with someone I wanted to spend time there with," he said.

"Oh, no?"

He chuckled. "What do you want to see?"

"Everything."

"Then everything it is," he assured me, tightening his arms around me.

* * *

Trey and I sat outside at a charming Paris café drinking *noisette*, the equivalent of a macchiato. I stared out at the Eiffel Tower in the distance. The clear blue sky behind it made it a thing of dreams for artists trying to capture its magnificence.

"I didn't mind staying there longer," Trey said.

The Tower was close enough to see from where we sat, but far enough away to avoid the tourists who may have been Savage Beasts fans. Trey loved his fans but had been great about making our time in Paris about him and me. I turned back to meet his gaze beneath his dark sunglasses. "It's fine. I'm just drinking it all in."

"And I'm drinking *you* all in," he teased.

I smiled before sipping my drink. "Can I ask you something?"

"Does it involve—"

"No," I said, stopping him from whatever inappropriate thing he planned to say next.

He sat back in his chair with a smirk, stretching his long legs out and crossing them at the ankles.

"It's actually work-related."

He threw back his head and groaned. "Way to kill a mood."

"Humor me for a minute."

"Go."

"Have you ever considered starting a charity for drug-addicted babies?"

He didn't respond, and I wished I could see his eyes beneath his sunglasses to know what he was thinking.

"You could use your celebrity status to call attention to a problem that some might not even know exists."

He turned his head, staring out at a group of students seemingly on a field trip. He still said nothing, remaining eerily silent.

My stomach dropped, and I suddenly regretted bringing it up. But now that I had, I was unsure how to stop. "The band donates to so many wonderful causes. I just wanted to be sure you were donating to something that means something to you." It was as if my mouth had a mind of its own. "You're so much more than just a drummer in a band. You're kind and caring and could be a voice for those who don't have one."

He'd yet to look back to me, and his continued silence had me cursing my big mouth.

"It was just a thought," I said. "If you hate the idea, you can just forget I ever brought it up."

"I don't hate the idea, Brie." He finally looked back to me. "I'd just feel more comfortable making an anonymous donation. I don't wanna be some posterchild for drug-addicted babies. The media would have a field day with it. Could you imagine them working in questions about it during interviews with the band? Sounds like a fucking nightmare."

Dammit. I hadn't thought of that. "I understand."

"Do you?"

"Of course. The press can be ruthless. They'd definitely back you into an uncomfortable corner. Not to mention the women who could come out of the woodwork claiming to be your birth mother."

He sat up and dragged his hands through his hair. "*Christ.* I hadn't even thought of that."

A long silence passed between us.

How had I not considered what a nightmare it could've been for Trey if the news about his past got out there? I prided myself on always thinking ahead—always anticipating impending shit shows. How had I not considered that?

"I have been thinking about giving back for a while now," he said. "I just didn't know how to go about it without bringing unwanted attention to myself. Will you look into it and bring me some options?"

"I can do that," I said, feeling more at ease that he'd actually considered it before. "Where were you born?"

"Las Vegas."

"No. I know that much. Which hospital?"

"Las Vegas General. Why?"

"I'd like to start by giving the NICU director there a call tomorrow. It's where you got your start and met your mom." Trey deserved to give other children the opportunities he had.

Trey stood up and rounded the table, pulling me to my feet. "Look at your wheels turning." He leaned in and instead of kissing my lips, he pressed kisses all over my face, causing me to giggle like a teenager. "I love…"

I stilled, my belly flipping over itself.

"…that you want to help me," Trey finished.

I released a breath. *Had I really thought he was going to say he loved me?* I couldn't be this far gone already. It was way too soon. "I'm always here to help."

"Yeah, but now you want to help because you like me," he teased.

"I never said I liked you."

He laughed. "You didn't have to. It's written all over your face."

"Is that so?"

He nodded. "Especially when my mouth's between your legs."

I dropped my head back and groaned. "You had to take it there, huh?"

"Oh, I definitely had to take it there," he laughed.

Treyton

The French crowd chanted our name as we waited backstage pre-show. The floor beneath our feet vibrated with the rumble of their cheers. If their enthusiasm was any indication, tonight's show was gonna be killer.

A hand came up and clasped the back of my shoulder. I looked over to find Z. "What's up, dude?"

"I could ask you the same question," he said.

"What's that mean?"

He shrugged the way only Z could, carrying more meaning in the shrug than his words would.

"Just ask what you want to ask," I said.

His brows shot up in question. "Brielle?"

"Life works in mysterious ways."

He scoffed. "You're not telling me something I don't know."

He'd fallen for Aubrey, an unlikely match, against all odds. And, not everyone was happy about it—including me. *Man, I was such a hypocrite.* "I'm sorry I didn't have your back with Aubrey."

"Do you have it now?" he asked.

"Obviously."

"Then, water under the bridge," Z said.

"I'm your best friend. I should've trusted that you knew what you were doing."

"Dude, *I* had no idea what I was doing," he assured me.

"Yeah, but I had no right to tell you who you should be with. I get that now. Because if any of you told me not to date Brie, I'd tell you to go fuck yourselves."

Z laughed. "So, you *are* dating Brielle?"

I shrugged. "I like her."

"That's a start. You don't like anyone."

I shoved his shoulder. "Asshole."

We both laughed, and I knew I had his blessing to be with Brie without judgment.

Brielle

I awoke in the middle of the night, reaching over and touching the cool hotel sheets beside me. Wherever Trey was, he'd been there for a while.

I slipped out of bed and pulled on shorts and Trey's T-shirt. I grabbed a keycard and slipped out of the room. I made my way down to the lobby, pretty certain that's where he'd gone.

Soft classical music greeted me as soon as I stepped off the elevator. I walked slowly over to the piano. Trey played with his eyes closed, caught up in the music like I'd seen him before. I sat on the bench beside him.

A smirk tipped his lips, though his eyes remained closed. "You smell like me."

I bumped him gently with my shoulder. "I like smelling like you."

Though his fingers didn't leave the keys, he opened his eyes and glanced to me. "What are you doing up?"

"I was lonely without you."

"Oh yeah?"

I nodded, enjoying the music he played effortlessly. "What brought you down here?"

He shrugged. "Just needed to play."

"It's beautiful."

"Thanks."

"You should add piano to the next album."

He shrugged again. "Nah. I don't need to share it."

I pushed myself to my feet. "I'm sorry, I just—"

"Sit your ass down."

I did.

"I don't mind sharing it with *you*, Brie. I just didn't wanna wake you to come down with me."

I pegged him with my eyes. "Next time wake me." I looked down at the keys and pressed one of them gently, adding my own sound to the song.

"Can you play?"

"No. My mom was the pianist. I just loved to sit and listen to her play. I wasn't a huge classical fan. I was more of her fan."

He eyed me sadly. "Now you can be my fan."

"I'm already your fan."

"Damn straight you are."

I laughed and so did he. "I bet you were a mama's boy."

"What would she think of her mama's boy now?" he mused.

"I think she'd be proud of all you've accomplished."

He bumped me gently with his shoulder. "You think so?"

I nodded. "I bet all your best qualities come from her."

"They do."

"And you'll pass those on to your own kids someday."

"Me with kids?" His eyes drifted, considering the notion.

"I've seen you with young fans. You're a natural. You'll be a great dad."

"I will be, won't I?"

I nodded, my confidence in him lighting up his face.

CHAPTER TWENTY-TWO

Brielle

Most tourists spent their week in Paris perusing art at the Louvre, enjoying a guided tour of Versailles, or taking selfies at the Eiffel Tower, pinching it from a distance to make it look small in the photo. Trey and I were no different. We'd done the touristy things, but we also sought out something equally as important to Trey before we left. A tattoo parlor.

"Does it hurt?" I asked as he lay on his side on the reclining chair while the tattoo artist penned a music note on his left arm on a small musical scale.

"Nothing I can't handle," he said. "Why? You thinking of getting something?"

"Nope," I answered matter-of-factly.

"Why not? You could get my name tattooed above your ass."

"*Right.*"

"Or, you could get a piercing. Just think how good a tongue ring would feel for me."

My thighs quivered at the thought of what he'd want me to do with a tongue ring, and I suddenly wished we were alone.

He lifted a brow and I knew he'd thought the same thing.

"Why don't you get my name above *your* ass?" I teased.

He scoffed at the idea. "Tell her," Trey said to the tattoo artist.

The tattoo artist glanced up from Trey's tattoo. "Rule number one," he said with a thick French accent. "Never get a female's name inked on your body."

"Why not?" I asked.

"It's the kiss of death," Trey said.

A pit formed in my stomach. It wasn't like I was thinking proposals and wedding bells when I was with Trey. But knowing, of all the things he had inked on his body, the idea of getting my name on him was that appalling told me he didn't view me as a staple in his life. And that sucked.

"You're done," the tattoo artist said a short time later. "Check it out."

Trey rolled off the chair and looked at his new tattoo in the mirror. He met my eyes in the mirror. "What do you think?"

I faked a grin, still unnerved by his comment. "Looks great."

He stared at me for a long time, his eyes narrowing on mine.

"Let me lather it up with ointment," the tattoo artist said, pulling Trey's attention away from mine.

We stepped out of the shop a little while later. Trey grabbed hold of my hand and walked me through the streets of Paris. Not the touristy areas, but the back roads with their quaint little shops for locals and the discreet homes stacked above them.

We walked in silence. The light breeze coasting through the narrow streets provided the only noise. Normally, I'd enjoy the silence. But the way Trey quickly dismissed putting my name on his body set me off-kilter.

I'd been floating on cloud nine since we started seeing each other, and that single moment in the tattoo shop just brought me back down to Earth, reminding me this thing between us might have an expiration date. "Trey?"

"Brie?"

"When we get back to the States…"

"You really want to do this here?" he asked.

"No. But I think I need to know what this is."

"What this is?" I could almost hear the irritation in his voice.

I nodded. "Are we just having fun and we'll go our separate ways once we get back, or is it something else?"

He stopped in the middle of the road and faced me, his expression a mix of frustration and anger. "What's this really about? You've been acting off since the shop."

"I just want to be prepared."

He dropped my hand and scrubbed his hand up and down the back of his head. "Brie, I'm not used to being with someone. You know that. I've never had to think past any single moment. Let alone think about someone else's feelings."

"I know. I just…" my voice trailed off and I suddenly felt as if I'd screwed everything up. *Wait.* I didn't screw anything up. He's the one who said it.

"I thought I've been doing a pretty good job of showing you I'm trying," he said.

"You have," I agreed.

He pulled up his sleeve and showed me his new tattoo covered in ointment and plastic wrap. "See this?"

I nodded.

"Do you know what note it is?"

I shook my head.

"It's a B flat."

My brows squished together, unsure why he was telling me this.

"It's a *B* flat," he said, accentuating the letter B.

Goosebumps scampered up my arms as my eyes widened. "You said no names."

His eyes softened. "I never said it couldn't represent a name." He wrapped his arms around me and held me to him. "This thing means something to me, Brie. Don't ever doubt that."

I said nothing, cursing my damn insecurities.

"If I say something that bothers you, like I guess I did back there, talk to me. Don't make me guess what's bothering you. Be upfront like you've always been. That's the Brie I fell for."

I froze, scared to move. Scared to breathe. Scared to think. He'd gotten a tattoo to represent me. And now, he'd just admitted he'd fallen for me.

"Yes, I just said that," he said. "Stop thinking so damn much, woman."

Trying to stifle a grin, I pulled back. "It's what I do. You know that."

"Then knock that shit out." He leaned forward and pressed his lips to mine.

Never had a kiss felt as right as his did in that moment.

CHAPTER TWENTY-THREE

Brielle

We arrived in Madrid a few days later, heading straight to the amusement park where the band was scheduled to make an appearance. Though the park had yet to open to the public, the band was greeted by applause by the VIP fans who won the opportunity to ride some of the rides with them.

The park's PR representative led all of us through the park to one of the biggest rollercoasters in Madrid.

"You going on it?" Trey asked.

I shook my head. "You saw me on the zip lines."

"Yeah," he said. "I saw you conquer your fear and kill it."

We stepped up to the massive coaster. My eyes took in the sky-high hills and death-defying drops. Fear grasped hold of me as I envisioned myself strapped into the coaster unable to escape.

Trey's hand slipped into mine. I tried to release it, but he tightened his grasp. "What are you doing?"

"People will see," I whispered.

"Are you embarrassed of me?" he asked.

"Completely. Have you looked in the mirror lately?"

He released my hand and slung his arm around my shoulders, pulling me into him. I laughed as he pressed his lips to my temple. "What are you gonna do now?"

I glanced around, quite a few eyes were on us. "You're breaking hearts as we speak."

"There's only one heart I'm worried about," he assured me.

"*Ohhhhh. You're good.*"

He smirked. "I am, aren't I?"

I spotted a teenager I'd seen earlier. Her eyes had been on Treyton since we arrived. Who could blame her? He looked hot in his torn jeans and black T-shirt. "Hey," I called to her.

She pointed to herself.

I nodded as I slipped out of Trey's hold. "Would you mind going on this ride with Treyton? He's a scaredy cat."

Excitement filled her features as she nodded.

I looked to Trey and winked.

"Oh, you think you're smart, don't you?" he whispered.

"I get you all the time. Your fans just want a little of your time."

He considered what I'd said. "You're all right, Brie Patrick."

My head flinched. "Just all right?"

He chuckled before turning to the girl and wrapping his arm over her shoulders. "You gonna hold my hand on the ride?" he asked her.

She giggled as they made their way onto the ride. Trey smiled at me as the ride attendant lowered the shoulder harness over him. Then his attention turned to his fan.

She deserved her time with Trey. She deserved to know what I knew. He was not only fun to be around, but also caring and generous—and did I mention hot? Because my man was extremely hot.

We moved from ride to ride, each bigger and faster than the last. I took photos of the guys and their fans. I didn't need to force Trey to choose fans to ride with. He sought one out for each ride. I posted the photos all over social media, some from the guys' accounts and some from the band's. Regardless, fans from all over the world were getting a firsthand account of what it was like to spend a day at an amusement park with their favorite band.

"Kozart's posts are getting double the likes," Aubrey informed me as we watched the guys get buckled into the free-fall ride.

"Oh, good. I tried to spread the posts around."

"You're really good at what you do," she said.

"Any publicist would do the same."

"You can admit you rock, you know?" she said.

I *was* good at my job. But only because I worked hard.

The fast trilling sound of a chain began. The guys and some fans were heaved four-hundred feet into the air on the ride. My stomach twisted into an uncomfortable knot just thinking about dropping from that height. Their legs dangled off the side of the ride as it sat waiting to drop. They were too far away to even differentiate who was who.

I lifted my phone and hit record just as the ride plummeted four-hundred feet. Screams came from all sides of the ride as the car they were harnessed into was yanked back up and dropped again like a yo-yo.

Aubrey laughed beside me as she snapped pictures. "Kozart's probably dying."

"What is it with these not-so-tough rock stars? Trey doesn't like heights either."

"The things you learn once they let you in." She said it lightly, but her eyes drifted away as if she was reminded of something she didn't care to share.

I wondered if she knew about Trey's rough start. I wondered if Z had confided in her, or if Trey had sworn him to secrecy.

"Let's go, Brielle," Cam said as he stepped off the free-fall ride with Trey and Z who followed feet behind looking like they'd been through the wringer. "You skipped all the big rides," Cam continued. "It's time we ride something more your speed."

"Oh, this has gotta be good," Trey said as he appeared beside me, looking a little steadier on his feet.

"You good?" I asked him.

"Better now," he said, dropping his arm around my shoulders and following Cam.

I should've known.

Cam brought us to kiddie land.

I lifted a brow at him. "Seriously?"

He smirked, then led us to the bumper cars.

"This is definitely more my speed," I assured him.

We all filed out onto the track, slipping into our own cars. There were only enough for the guys, Aubrey, BJ, and me. But the fans seemed content watching us as we belted ourselves in, and our colorful cars whirred to life.

Before I could even find my first target, someone slammed into me from behind. My body was jostled around as I glanced over my shoulder. Cam howled with delight. Until, Trey slammed into him from the side, cutting off his laughter.

I smiled, as they both went after each other. I drove around in a big circle, trying to avoid all the melee in the middle of the floor.

"Don't even think you're getting away unscathed, Brielle," Z shouted as he took off after me.

I swerved, thinking that was smarter than driving in a straight line, but Z slammed into my side, sending my car flying sideways and my body bouncing around. I laughed as I looked to him. He smiled, and it was the first time in a long time that I could see he didn't hate me anymore. And it felt good.

I was finally part of their family, and I'd never wanted to be a part of something more in my entire life.

CHAPTER TWENTY-FOUR

Treyton

"Where's Brielle?" I asked BJ as our van to the venue took off from the hotel without her in it.

"She asked me to take care of things at the venue," he said as we pulled out of the parking lot. "She had something to do at the hotel."

Something to do? I'd been with her only an hour before and she hadn't said anything. That was unlike her. She always ran our pre-show events—the control freak that she was.

"She's with Aubrey," Z added, seeing the concern on my face.

The last time she disappeared, things had taken a turn for the worse in Hungary. And we all know how that turned out.

At the venue, BJ lined us up for our meet and greets. I carried out my duties, greeting the Spanish fans, and smiling for way too many photos. And as much as I tried to be present for all these fans who'd waited to meet us, I'd be lying if I said my mind wasn't on Brie and where she was the entire time.

"One more pair," BJ informed us. "I hear they're your biggest fans in the world," he said before walking out of the meet and greet room to get the last two fans.

I pulled out my phone to send a quick text to Brie.

"Who you texting?" Brie asked.

I glanced up. My eyes nearly popped out of their sockets. Brie and Aubrey entered the meet and greet area, practically twins in their tiny cutoffs and Savage Beasts T-shirts. Brie looked like a fucking model with her hair in loose curls and her legs for days in ankle boots. "What the hell?"

She tucked her lips, stopping herself from smiling.

I stalked toward her, not caring who saw, and lifted her right off her feet. "You look so damn hot."

She laughed, and I loved that I was the one to bring it out of her.

"I've got five minutes. What do you say we find someplace to be alone?" I shifted my hips so she could feel what she'd done to me.

"Stop it," she whispered.

"I can't."

"Get a room," Marcus said.

We both peeked over to see the band standing there staring at us together. I guess I didn't blame them. It was definitely the first time we'd shown affection in front of anyone.

"You two look hot together," Aubrey said.

"You two are *together*?" Cam asked, completely stunned by the revelation.

We all rolled our eyes, knowing he really hadn't caught on yet.

I tilted my head and pressed my lips to Brie's for all to see. She laughed against my mouth, probably embarrassed that I wasn't holding back in front of everyone. I pulled back an inch. "How do you expect me to perform with you looking like this?"

"Aubrey thought it would be fun," she explained, keeping her voice down now that people were staring.

"Fun is definitely not the word for what this is." I

pulled my head back some more and stared at her in my arms.

"Put me down. I want my picture with the band."

"Yeah?"

She nodded.

"Fine. But you're gonna stand right by the side of the stage during the show so I can see you, you understand?"

Amused, she shook her head.

I lowered her to her feet but didn't release her as the band crowded around us. BJ snapped a bunch of photos with his phone.

"Cam, your hand better not be on Brie's ass," I said through a smile.

"She doesn't seem to mind," Cam responded.

Everyone laughed as we moved apart. I pulled Brie back to me and dropped my forehead to hers. "I'm taking these clothes off you later."

"Deal."

"Very slowly," I assured her.

"Okay."

"With my teeth."

Laughter tumbled out of her.

God dammit. When she laughed like that, I swore I'd never need another girl's laugh in my life ever again.

Brielle

Trey and I strolled through the hotel lobby hand in hand. Their show had been amazing and the Spanish crowd loved every moment of their set, especially "Fireflies." Z stopped singing with his microphone extended out, and the entire audience sang along.

"Brielle," my father's stony voice echoed through the lobby.

A cold chill shot up my spine, and I immediately dropped Trey's hand. I turned to find my father, in his black suit and gray tie, approaching.

He stopped in front of us, making no attempt to hug me.

"What are you doing here?" I asked.

His eyes jumped between Trey and me. Then his narrowed eyes took in my outfit.

Shit.

"You said you were needed out here. Is this what you've been doing? Running around Madrid looking like a slut?"

I gasped, more embarrassed that he'd said it in front of Trey than that he'd actually said it. He never held back when it came to his thoughts—especially the hurtful ones.

"Excuse me, Mr. Patrick," Trey said, his jaw clenched. "Brielle is gorgeous. If she chose to dress like one of our fans tonight for fun, she doesn't deserve to be called names. Especially by her father. I think you owe her an apology."

My father scoffed. "Excuse me…" he tipped his head, as if he didn't know Trey's name.

"It's Treyton," Trey said, disdain dripping from his tone.

"Well, excuse me *Treyton* for calling it like I see it."

Ticking began in Trey's jaw. I quickly grasped his arm, letting him know I was okay. I looked to my father. "Why are you here?"

"You haven't returned my calls."

"The only thing that could warrant you flying overseas to see me would be the death of my mother. But that already happened and it took you two days to get to me."

His face grew colder. "That was uncalled for."

"So was this trip. But we both know the real reason you're here has nothing to do with me. What kind of publicist would I be if I wasn't up on current events? Martina Suarez is getting married tomorrow. Anyone who's anyone will be at the A-lister's wedding."

He grabbed hold of my arm.

"Whoa," Trey said, stepping forward. "Let go of her."

My father scoffed as he released his grip on me. "So, not only are you dressing like a whore, you're dating your client."

"It's none of your business," I said.

A devious grin slipped across his face. "Oh, on the contrary. It most definitely is."

"You haven't cared who I've dated since…ever."

"Yes, but now you're breaking the non-fraternization policy you signed when I hired you."

My face fell slack. "I don't remember signing that."

"Then I'll assume you don't know the consequence."

Another cold shiver raced up my spine.

He smiled in a way that only a heartless bastard could smile. "You're fired."

The floor seemingly dropped from beneath my feet.

"*Or…*" he continued, eyeing Trey. "End the relationship with your client."

"That's not fair," I said.

"You're right," my father continued. "We can't leave Savage Beasts without a publicist. Arthur can take over for you—just like he did after you took it upon yourself to terminate the contract with Flow Houz." The sugary sweet way he added that told me his anger had been brewing.

"We want Brie," Trey said.

"I'm sorry," my father said. "Brielle signed a contract then broke it. What kind of business would I be running if I showed nepotism and allowed my daughter to break a rule? She needs to be held to the same standard as all of my other employees."

"She's not your other employees," Trey said. "She's your daughter."

My mind spun and a high-pitched ringing pierced my ears. Was my father really doing this? Was he really giving an ultimatum—a no-win ultimatum—to his own daughter? After all I'd been through trying to prove myself to him, was he really going to force my hand to either break up with Trey or dispose of me like yesterday's trash?

Trey glared at my father as he grabbed hold of my hand. "I'll be talking to Z about this."

"Every person is replaceable, Son," my father said.

"I'm not your son"

My father's eyes took him in. "Clearly." He turned away from us and walked away.

My legs trembled beneath me. My knees threatened to give out. Had I really signed that policy? Was he really making me choose?

"We won't let this happen," Trey promised as he pulled me into his side.

"I don't think it's up to you," I said.

CHAPTER TWENTY-FIVE

Treyton

I left Brie in her room after she'd finally fallen asleep. I pounded on BJ's door. He pulled it open, and I stormed in.

"Problem?" he asked.

I leaned against the dresser, crossing my arms to stop my hands from shaking. "Brielle just got an ultimatum."

"What?"

"Her asshole father showed up here and gave her a choice. Either resign since she broke a non-fraternization policy by dating me or break it off with me."

BJ's face scrunched.

"I need you to fix it."

"Fix it?" he asked. "If she broke her contract with him, it has nothing to do with us."

"She works for us. And she loves working for us. I can't make her quit for me."

"Our contract is with Artists Limited, not Brielle," he explained.

"Then fire them."

"You want to fire Brielle?"

I shook my head, frustration emanating from my body. "No. Fire the company and we'll hire her on her own. I don't want her working for that asshole anyway."

"Treyton, we have a contract with the firm. It's legally binding. If they've done nothing to warrant us rescinding the contract, we could owe them a lot of money."

"Can we get out of the contract legally?"

"I have no idea."

"I need you to look into it."

A smile spread across BJ's face.

"How can you smile right now?"

"It's nice to see you worried about her. She's spent a lot of time cleaning up after you and making sure you were okay. It's nice to see you returning the favor. I think it's a good thing. You and her."

"Dude." I pushed off the dresser. "I need you to help make this right."

He saluted me. "I'll see what I can do."

Brielle

I awoke alone in the pitch-black hotel room, hoping it had all been a terrible dream. But nausea in my stomach and the ache in my temples told me it hadn't been. Trey wasn't there. I assumed he'd taken off for the piano once I'd fallen asleep. I slipped out of bed, still wearing the outfit I'd been so excited to wear for him. Now I felt like the whore my father saw me as.

How did he still have so much power over me? Why hadn't I severed ties with him a long time ago? Deep down I knew why. This wasn't about the firm. This wasn't about me taking over one day. This was because he was my last connection to my mother. Once he was out of my life, I had no family left.

I grabbed my keycard, hurried out of the room, and made my way to the elevator. Instead of pressing the button for the lobby, I jammed my finger into the button for the top floor. I knew that's where he'd be. He never stayed anywhere but the penthouse like the big shot he thought he was. Once the elevator came to a stop and the doors spread apart, I trudged down the hallway and knocked on the door. It took a couple of minutes, but footsteps shuffled behind it. He paused, and I assumed he was checking the peephole first. His scoff carried through the door.

My stomach churned, but I held my composure, standing with my spine straight and my chin up—the way I'd seen him do it for my entire life.

The door opened and my father stood before me in a robe, his eyes assessing my outfit with disdain once again. "I see you dressed up for me."

Keeping my composure, I brushed by him, moving into the dining room. "I need you to sit down."

"I don't think you're in any position to give orders."

"We need to talk." I pulled out a chair at the dining room table and sat, hoping he'd follow my lead.

He took his time circling the table before actually sitting in the chair across from me.

"I want that non-fraternization policy retracted."

He cocked his head. "Come again?"

"You heard me." I stared him right in the eyes. "I'm your daughter. I have a job I love and someone I care about who cares about me and treats me the way I should be treated. Are you really going to take one of those away from me?"

"I'm not taking anything away from you."

A flicker of hope sparked inside me.

"*You* signed the contract," he continued. "Now, *you* have the choice."

I wanted to jump across the table and hurt him the way he was hurting me, but I drew a deep breath and finally asked the question I'd needed to ask my whole life. "Have you ever loved anyone?"

His face scrunched. "What kind of question is that?"

"Have you ever felt the kind of love for another person that you feel for yourself?"

"This is not the way to go about keeping your job," he assured me.

"I'm being serious. I never understood how you could leave Mom and me for a job. How you could stay married, but not want anything to do with either of us because your job and those celebrities were so much more important to you. The only possible thing I can come up with is that you're incapable of love."

He said nothing, staring at me with his lips in a tight line.

"I'm falling in love with Treyton. He is so much more than anyone knows." My father's silence, and my desperation to keep Trey *and* my job, urged me on. "He was born addicted to drugs. He was born to someone who couldn't love him either. But then he found someone who could. The woman who rocked babies in the nursery. Holding him in her arms was all it took for her to fall in love with him. She just knew it was meant to be." My eyes lowered to my lap. "He lost her at ten, just like I lost Mom." I paused for a long moment before looking back up. I hoped to see something in my father's face, but it remained unaffected by anything I'd said. "Treyton and I are so different, but it's the small similarities that bond us. We care about each other which makes us the lucky ones. I want to believe you wouldn't wish unhappiness on me."

"I don't wish unhappiness on you, Brielle," he finally said. "But in our world, we sign contracts. So now you have a choice. Pick the option that will make you happy. I'm not standing in your way."

My shoulders wilted. Of course he was standing in my way. And nothing I said or did would change his mind. That's why he was so good at his job. He'd hear anyone out and let them feel heard, then he'd crush them and their dreams.

* * *

"Jesus Christ." Trey rushed to meet me as I stepped into the hotel room. "I've been calling you like a crazy person. Where'd you go?"

I walked over to the bed and sat.

"Oh fuck. Did you…?"

I nodded regrettably. "I needed to see if he would hear me out. I had to try."

"And?"

I shook my head.

Trey sat down beside me. The dipping of the bed under his weight pulled me closer to him, and he wrapped his arm around me. "We'll get this figured out."

"Will we? Because the way I see it, I have two options."

A long silence passed between us, and I couldn't help wondering what Trey was thinking. Was he realizing dating me was turning out to be more trouble than it was worth?

"He's even more of an asshole than I imagined," he finally said.

"Yup."

"Why don't you just tell him we broke it off? Lie to him."

"I'm no good at lying. I'd be waiting for him to find out. You know, like waiting for that other shoe to inevitably drop." I dragged in a deep breath. "Can we just sleep? I need your arms around me. And I need to not think about this for the rest of the night."

Trey clearly wanted to get this figured out, but instead of pushing me, he stood us up and pulled down the comforter. I climbed in first and he followed, pulling the comforter over us as he nestled in behind me and wrapped me up in his arms like I'd asked. He buried his nose in my hair and whispered, "Sleep, Brie. We'll figure this out in the morning."

"Promise?" I asked.

"Promise," he lied, like he knew I needed him to.

And I loved him for it.

CHAPTER TWENTY-SIX

Treyton

Someone knocking on the door pulled me from a restless sleep a little after six in the morning. Brie stirred in my arms where she'd slept just as restlessly all night. I slipped my arms out from around her and rolled off the bed, hurrying to the door so whoever it was didn't wake her.

I pulled it open to find Z standing there glaring at me.

"What's wrong?" I stepped into the hallway and stuck my foot in between the door and door jamb to keep it from locking me out.

"Have you checked your phone?" Z asked.

"No. You just woke me up."

"Who'd you talk to?" Z asked.

I scrubbed my hands up and down my face to wake myself up. "Talk to about what?"

He cocked his head.

"Dude, you're not making any sense. What's going on?"

"Did you tell Brielle about your shit?"

The hair on the back of my neck stood on end, knowing exactly what he meant by those words.

"It's out there," he explained. "People know about your past."

It was as if I'd just been doused with a cold bucket of water. I was fairly certain any color had drained from my face. Z and I had a pact. Neither of us talked about the way we grew up or met. No one knew about the shitty lives we'd been born into. So, if they knew my shit, they knew his. *God dammit.* "I only told Brie."

Disappointment shone heavy in Z's eyes. "Dude?"

"She wouldn't put it out there."

Z kept staring, and I felt myself needing to plead my case. Needing to convince him she was innocent.

"She wanted the band to start a charity or make a donation to the hospital where I was born," I explained. "I told her it needed to be done anonymously and she agreed."

He stared at me, and the longer he stared, the more I questioned my decision to open up to her.

"She knew not to bring my name into it," I explained.

"She's proven she can't be trusted in the past," Z argued.

And while I wanted to sucker-punch my best friend for saying that, I also saw the truth in it. She *had* proven she'd take things into her own hands when she thought it was important for the band. If she brought up my past, she'd be putting the band at the top of news feeds. It was her job to keep us relevant. Because relevancy in the PR world was more important than anything.

Even me.

Dammit.

I tunneled my fingers through my hair, hating myself in that moment. Z never wanted the word out there that his parents were drug addicts and dealers who abandoned him. And he had every right to want to keep his business private. What he hadn't banked on was me opening my damn mouth.

Fuuuuuuuck.

"Has your name been mentioned?" I asked, terrified to hear his answer.

He shook his head. "Not yet. Just waiting for it, though."

If our past got out there, there was no way to erase it. It would be what people thought of when they saw us. Maybe they wouldn't say it, but they'd be thinking it. The crack baby and the kid who was abandoned by drug dealers. It would always be there, like the black cloud we both worked so hard to escape. "I fucked up."

Z said nothing. He was pissed I'd betrayed his trust. I could see it in the way his eyes avoided mine.

"I thought Brie was different."

He scoffed. "Really? Because I've heard leopards don't change their spots."

I dropped my head back against the door. "I should've known better."

Z said nothing. He wasn't the type to console someone when they were in the wrong.

And I *was* in the wrong for opening my mouth. But how could I have known she'd betray me? "I'm sorry I trusted her."

The door behind me yanked open causing me to shuffle forward.

Brie stepped into the hallway in jeans and a T-shirt pulling her luggage. She looked me dead in the eyes. "You definitely shouldn't have trusted her. But don't worry. *She's* leaving." She walked down the hallway to the stairwell, not waiting for the elevator.

I didn't try to stop her. I was way too pissed to even consider it. *She'd* betrayed *me.* Not the other way around. I'd been a fool to let her in. A fool who thought maybe I'd found someone I could invest time in. Someone who'd be a staple in my life. She'd known me for five years and still took a chance on me, with all my flaws and epic screw-ups. Now I realized it was me who'd taken the chance on her. And it clearly bit me in the ass.

There was no bouncing back from something like this.

She'd betrayed me and my best friend for the last time.

We were done.

CHAPTER TWENTY-SEVEN

Brielle

"We're beginning our final descent and should be arriving at LAX in just a few minutes," the pilot's voice informed us over the cabin intercom. "Be sure to check that all your belongings are packed up. It's been a pleasure flying with you."

A pleasure? Nothing about the fifteen-hour flight had been a pleasure. Not the perpetual pit in the bottom of my stomach. Not the crying kid two rows back. Not the thoughts whirling through my head making sleep impossible. Not the uncertainty I now had about what came next for me. Nothing.

I'd needed time to think on the flight. Time to wrap my head around what happened back in Madrid. Time to put myself in Trey's shoes. But I still came up short.

Trey and Z had each other's backs when times got tough. But no one had my back. No one let me explain. They both just assumed the worst of me.

They had to know by now that I'd never want to intentionally hurt either of them. I wasn't a malicious person. And I'd never betray someone's trust. But from the conversation I'd overheard between the two of them, they didn't believe that.

At least now I knew.

Now I was aware, before my feelings got any deeper,

that Treyton Collins was a coward. At the first sign of trouble, he turned on me.

He'd told me the one thing he wanted in this world was a family. I guess that was a lie. Because you didn't turn on the people you cared about. You didn't just stop caring about them just because you thought they messed up.

As the plane slowly descended, I dropped my head back and closed my eyes, having absolutely no idea what came next for me.

Treyton

The guys and I sat at a large table inside an Italian radio studio wearing headphones and answering on-air questions about the tour. BJ looked on from outside the glass window with our new publicist Arthur—a real tool in a suit.

"So, what can the fans expect for your next album?" the DJ asked with a heavy Italian accent.

We all looked to Z who did the majority of our songwriting.

"More of what the fans want," he said. "Some slower ballads to go with the rock that gets fans ready to rage. You know, more of what they've come to expect from us."

"*Fantastico*," the DJ said before his eyes moved slowly to me. "Treyton. A story recently broke about your unfortunate past."

My stomach churned like I'd eaten something rotten. Beads of sweat built on my hairline. I'd been dreading this moment. And now it was here. What was he looking for? My sob story? Tears? A witty response? The only positive was no stories about Z's past had yet to surface.

"Glad you turned out so well, *amico*," the DJ continued without a question. "Some people just aren't meant to be parents."

"Yeah," I said, relieved he didn't intend to pry. Didn't intend to make me relive it for his ratings.

But as he turned to Cam, prepared to ask him a question, Brie's words about being a voice for those who didn't have one played through my mind. And as much as I just wanted him to move on, I suddenly felt compelled to say more.

"I'm not sure how much of an epidemic it is here," I began. "But in the States, there are so many children born to addicts who don't get adopted. And all they need are some caring people to love them. If anyone out there feels like they or someone they know could be those people, please reach out to your child services department to see how you may be able to help."

I glanced to Z who nodded subtly.

"I was one of the lucky ones," I continued. "My adoptive parents were amazing. They introduced me to music. Without them, I don't know where I'd be."

The DJ smiled. "Thank God they did because you are pure magic on those drums."

And just like that, he turned to Cam and asked a question about bungee-jumping, which he'd done that morning.

I looked back to Z who nodded his approval. Was he thinking what I was thinking? Our past. Our unfortunate circumstances. They didn't garner us pity. They garnered us anger for the shit we'd been through.

Z and I had made our pact when we were teenagers. That was a time when we were rebellious, angry, and didn't want people knowing our business. But now we were in the public eye. Now we were looked up to by kids *and* adults. What was the point of lying about where we came from? By omitting that personal information, we'd been lying to our fans—the people who bought our music and paid to see us in concert. We may not have owed anything to the kids we went to high school with, but we did owe our fans the truth. And the truth was we had a shitty start to life, more-so Z than me since I didn't even remember my birth mother. But that didn't define us. That made us the strong sons of bitches we were.

CHAPTER TWENTY-EIGHT

Brielle

I stepped into the office I had been away from for almost two months. Its floor to ceiling windows cast bright sunlight over the sleek white desk, side tables, and chairs lining the waiting room.

"Hi Brielle," Irene greeted me with a smile from her seat behind the front desk. "Welcome back."

"Is my father in?" I asked, walking by without stopping.

"He's in with a client," she called.

I passed some of my colleagues en route to the big office in the corner.

"Welcome back, Brielle," a few of them called as I passed by their offices.

I said nothing, my attention remained solely on the closed door in front of me. I didn't bother knocking. I threw the door open and swept right in.

The client across from my father at his desk twisted in his seat. Flow Houz. His eyes rounded.

"Brielle? What are you doing here?" my father asked, more pissed that I'd interrupted a meeting than surprised I was home.

"I've made a decision. And I thought I'd bring you the news in person." My eyes flashed to Flow. "But imagine my delight to find *you* here."

"'Sup," he said, slouched in his seat and avoiding eye contact.

"Sup? That's all you got?" I asked. "Because from what I heard, you had a lot to say about me when I wasn't there. What was it you said about my tits and ass?"

"Don't know what you're talking about," he grumbled.

"Brielle!" my father chided. "I'll meet with you when I'm finished here."

I crossed my arms. "No."

His head shot back. "I beg your pardon?"

"I said *no*." I pointed at Flow. "We should have terminated his contract the second he disrespected me. The way he spoke about me was not okay, and not doing something about it immediately was on me. But I won't make that mistake again." I looked back to my father. "I quit."

Flow went to stand. "Maybe I should go."

"No," my father said.

"Great idea," I said.

Flow hurried out of the office, closing the door behind him.

You could've cut the silence in the office with a knife. But I was beyond letting my father be in charge of everything. "I quit this job, and I quit being your daughter."

My father leaned back in his seat and crossed his arms, saying nothing.

"You win. You get what you wanted all along. I no longer work here, and I want nothing to do with you. You never treated me the way I deserved to be treated. The way *Mom* treated me. But still, I tried to prove to you that I was worthy of your respect." A humorless laugh shot out of me. "For what? You were never going to hand over this business to me. And you were never going to love me. You betraying me by running to the press with Trey's story was the final straw. Now you not only messed with my life, but you messed with someone else's. Someone who didn't ask to get caught up in this mess. So, I am bowing out. I put up a valiant effort. But enough is enough." I looked up at the ceiling. "Mom. I finally did what you weren't able to do. I'm walking away on *my* terms." I spun away from him and walked out of his office.

I exited Artists Limited with a smile on my face and the giant boulder I'd been carrying on my shoulders for far too long lifted.

Treyton

I smiled my way through one of our last meet and greets, amped to get on stage in Monaco. Arthur escorted in two gorgeous statuesque women. They weren't the normal fans decked out in Savage Beasts' wear. These two were dressed to the nines, their high-heels making them taller than all of us.

Arthur introduced Adriana and Victoria as runway models for a famous designer, like we couldn't already tell their beauty paid their bills. "*Bonjour*," they greeted us, cheek skimming us like most models did so they didn't mess up their lipstick. "Pleasure to meet you," they said with French accents, as they made their way down the line.

"Photo time," Arthur announced, every word out of his mouth making me cringe.

The models squeezed in under each of my arms, smelling of expensive perfume as a bunch of photos were snapped. Arthur would be posting those every-where. And I'd definitely be linked to one—if not both of them—by the morning.

"Good to meet you," Adriana said, as she leaned in again for a cheek kiss and tucked something into my back pocket.

"You too," I said as she followed Victoria out of the room.

Once they'd left, Cam and Marcus fanned themselves down with their hands. Z laughed at them, probably glad Aubrey hadn't been there.

I slipped the paper out of my pocket. Couldn't say it was the first time I'd had a phone number passed my way. But it was the first time since splitting with Brie that anyone had tried.

There was no denying Adriana was gorgeous. But the attention from a beautiful woman would not fill the perpetual emptiness I'd been feeling in my chest. No matter how much I wanted it to. And as much as it pissed me off to admit it, Brie betraying me slayed me.

"Last meet and greet of the night," Arthur called before walking out to retrieve our final two fans.

A flashback of Brie and Aubrey surprising us as our biggest fans flashed in my mind. The happiness I felt in that moment had quickly been replaced by hatred when Z told me what she'd done. That's how it had always been with Brie. Great highs and even greater lows.

I shook off the thoughts and prepared for our last two fans.

A man in his late forties in a Savage Beasts T-shirt holding the arm of a teenage boy with special needs entered the room. I couldn't take my eyes off the boy who needed his father's arm for support to walk. He and his dad shook Z's hand first. The boy didn't make eye contact with Z, but the joy on his face said everything he was clearly unable to convey with words. The dad said something that made Z look over at me. His lips twisted regrettably, and I had no idea what to make of it.

The father and son approached Marcus and Cam, who stood between Z and me. They spoke for a couple of minutes.

When they reached me, the man introduced himself, and then his son, Matteo. Matteo didn't look at me, but the smile on his face and quiet grunts told me he was happy to be there.

"Matteo's one of *your* biggest fans," his father explained. "We were so happy you went public with your story. Matteo was born to an addict. He had multiple complications and is nonverbal as a result. But his face lights up and he bobs his head anytime we play your music. Especially when the drum solos play."

"That's awesome," I said, not sure if I should touch Matteo or not. I hated myself in that moment. I hated that I escaped unscathed while people like Matteo weren't as fortunate. "You adopted him?" I asked his father.

He nodded. "When he was just a baby."

I turned to Arthur. "Grab me some merchandise for my friend Matteo here."

Arthur took off and I turned back to Matteo. "Do you have a favorite song?" I knew he couldn't respond with words, so I held up my thumb then turned it down, showing him how he could answer me.

He lifted his hand and gave me a thumbs up.

"I bet it's 'Crossover,'" I said.

Matteo turned his thumb down.

"What's wrong with 'Crossover'?" I laughed, feigning disappointment.

His father laughed. "Think first album."

"Oh, I know…'Midnight.'"

Matteo's eyes lifted to the ceiling as he turned his thumb up.

"Z and I wrote that together when we were around your age. And it's still my favorite, too. How old are you, Matteo?"

He looked to his dad.

"Sixteen," he answered for him.

"I bet you get all the girls," I said.

Matteo snorted and he clapped his hands excitedly.

His dad and I laughed, loving his reaction.

"I'll take that as a yes," I said. "Would you like a picture?"

Matteo's dad nodded and Matteo flashed a thumbs up.

"How about one with the band and then one with just their amazing drummer?" I teased.

Matteo's dad laughed. "That would mean the world to Matteo."

What he didn't realize—what *I* hadn't realized until that moment—was that it would mean the world to me, too.

CHAPTER TWENTY-NINE

Brielle

I hurried into my bedroom and grabbed my ringing phone from the dresser. I didn't recognize the number. But, I'd been putting my résumé out there, so I didn't want to miss any calls from prospective employers. I lifted the phone to my ear. "Hello?"

"Ms. Patrick?"

"Yes."

"This is Elaine Newberry, neonatal intensive care unit coordinator at Las Vegas General."

My heart wilted. I'd forgotten I called her regarding an anonymous donation. "Yes. Hi. Thanks for returning my call."

"We were delighted to hear that your client may have a donation for our unit. I'd love for you to come in and see how we run the NICU and all the advances we've made over the last few years so you'll know where your client's money would be going."

I stood there with my mind reeling. She sounded so excited. I couldn't bear to tell her that the money was no longer coming.

"When can I expect you?" she asked.

"Oh, I…" *Dammit.* "Friday?"

"Friday would be amazing. Let's say noon?

What am I doing? "Sure."

"I look forward to meeting you. God bless you and your client."

"Thank you," I said before disconnecting the call.

What the hell was I doing? I no longer had money to offer and any of my own money was socked away until I got another job. I could make a small donation, but the type of money the band would have donated would actually have benefited the hospital. When she saw the meager amount I'd be able to give, she'd be upset I wasted her time.

But I couldn't say no. Maybe the masochist in me needed to see where Trey was born. Maybe the optimist inside of me hoped he still intended to make the donation.

***

My high heels clicked as I hurried to the fifth floor in my gray pencil skirt and satin pink blouse. My hair was pulled back and my glasses were in place as I stepped up to the glass window outside the neonatal intensive care unit on Friday.

Babies in clear plastic incubator beds were lined up on display sleeping, fussing, or crying. Most were snuggled tightly in their swaddles and others were attached to machines with tubes beneath their tiny noses or IVs tightly wrapped around their legs. What they all had in common was they were tiny. Like two to three pounds tiny.

Two older women in scrubs rocked babies in rocking chairs, while nurses fed some with small bottles of formula.

A woman in a suit stepped out of the door and greeted me. "Ms. Patrick?"

"Brielle," I said, reaching out my hand and shaking hers.

"Hi Brielle, I'm Elaine Newberry. So glad you could make it."

Would she still be glad when I broke the bad news to her?

"Come," she said. "I want you to see the NICU." She walked me around the area, showing me the family room where the families with babies in the NICU spent time with their babies. She walked me through the new auditorium where doctors held conferences discussing the latest advances in neonatal care. Then, we circled back around to the nursery. She pointed out how many babies required incubators and ventilators. My heart broke for the innocent little fighters.

"Where are all the moms?" I asked, noting only nurses and volunteer rockers in there. "Don't they want to be here with their babies?"

"Many of them come in at some point during the day. Their premature babies are here for months sometimes before they are released, so these parents need to work while they await their baby's homecoming. Unfortunately, the other babies have birth parents who signed off on parental rights."

My gut clenched. That's what Trey's birth mother had done.

"Are those babies awaiting adoption?"

Her eyes lost their excitement. "The majority will end up in foster care. Placing babies who are born addicted to drugs isn't easy. They're more irritable, have birth defects, are prone to seizures, and there is no way to know to what extent they'll require long term care once they're grown. It's a giant risk for adoptive parents. One they don't necessarily want to take."

I nodded. "I'm aware. That was the reason for my client's donation. He was born addicted and was actually adopted by one of the women who rocked babies here."

Elaine's eyes regained some excitement. "Really?"

I nodded. "He wanted to give back."

"You can't imagine how much we need donations and outside funding to give these babies what they need moving forward. It's never an easy road for the foster families or adoptive parents. There are a number of long-term issues that come with being addicted to drugs in the womb when all vital organs are developing."

"Could I hold one of the babies?" I had no idea what possessed me to ask.

A smile tugged at the corners of her lips. "Would you like to?"

I nodded, suddenly having an urge like no other to bring some comfort to these babies. They deserved to be held and rocked like every other baby who had loving parents.

"Let's get you sanitized. We have scrubs if you don't want to risk messing up that pretty shirt."

"I'm not worried about a shirt."

Within a few minutes, I was in a rocking chair and a tiny baby was placed into my arms. A tube was attached beneath her precious little nose. She was so light. I could barely distinguish her from the blanket she was swaddled in, and the knitted pink hat on her head almost covered her entire face.

"She was born addicted to heroin," Elaine informed me. "Her mother took off as soon as she could. We have The Safe Haven Infant Protection Act here in Nevada. Parents have the right to abandon their babies with no punishment."

My stomach turned at the thought of someone deserting this innocent little baby. "Will she be okay?" I asked.

"Hard to tell what the future holds. But right now, she's doing exactly what we need her to do."

I stared down at the sleeping baby. "She looks perfect."

Elaine smiled. "I have some things to do. You're welcome to stay here and rock her for as long as you like."

"Thank you," I whispered, not wanting to wake the sleeping baby. "I'll come find you when I'm done."

I watched Elaine leave, then my eyes were pulled back to the baby in my arms. Her little eyes twitched behind her thin—almost translucent—eyelids. I rubbed my thumb over her little chin. Her skin was so smooth and warm. The scent of baby powder drifted off her as I rocked the chair back and forth. I'm not sure how long I sat with her in my arms, but her eyes eventually opened.

"Hello there," I whispered.

Trey told me drug-addicted babies didn't make eye contact. I watched closely, wondering where her eyes would go. She was too little to focus, but I began to hum "Rock-a-Bye Baby," and she strained to look toward the sound.

A younger nurse shuffled by me and smiled.

"Excuse me?" I whispered to her.

She turned back.

"Does she have a name?"

She shook her head regrettably before walking away.

I inched closer to the baby and whispered, "I'm gonna call you...Claire."

She shifted in my arms.

"I'll take that as you like it," I said to her.

The same nurse returned a little later carrying a bottle. "Would you like to feed her?"

My eyes widened. "I don't know how."

She grinned. "It's easy." She held the bottle to Claire's mouth at a slanted angle.

I grabbed hold of the bottle, and Claire was already sucking the formula out.

"Once she drinks half an ounce," the nurse continued. "Just hold her against your chest and rub her back. She'll give you a little burp and you can continue feeding her half an ounce at a time until she won't take any more."

"Okay," I said, looking as worried as I felt.

"You'll be fine," she assured me before walking off to tend to a crying baby across the room.

I held the bottle and watched Claire suck away at it, knowing how important the formula was for her little body. I checked the measurements on the side of the bottle. Once half an ounce had disappeared, I pulled the bottle from her mouth. Her little lips kept sucking even without the bottle there. I placed my finger in its place to stop the movement, but she sucked away at the tip of my finger.

"Hold on, little Claire. I just need to burp you." I picked her up and placed her against my heart, rubbing her back in tiny circles. It took a minute but a small hiccup came out. I wasn't sure at first if that was the burp, but once she began squirming and no other sound came, I settled her back into my arms and gave her the bottle, which she took willingly.

After the formula had disappeared and Claire had burped multiple times, she fell back asleep in my arms. Leaving her was going to be difficult. It wasn't like I'd just been babysitting and someone was coming to claim her. She was there until she was strong enough to go to foster care. The thought wore on me, even after I had given her back to the nurse and she'd been placed in her bed.

I walked to Elaine's office down the hall and stopped in her open doorway.

"How'd it go?" Elaine asked as she found me standing there.

"You have a wonderful facility and everyone is so nice."

Her hopeful eyes stared at me, awaiting my news.

"I'm going to need to speak to my client to see how he'll be able to assist."

She nodded, and I could see the disappointment in her eyes. She wanted me to write the check right then. And I completely understood.

"I'll be in Las Vegas for the weekend. Would it be okay if I came back? I've taken a liking to Claire."

Her brows dipped. "Claire?"

My cheeks heated. "That's just what I was calling her. It seemed fitting."

She smiled a sad smile, likely thinking the same thing as me. How could a woman give birth to a child and leave it with nothing—not even a name? "Please come back. We'd love to have you."

"Thank you." I moved away from her door and made my way down the hallway, stopping to peek into the window of the nursery. Claire was still asleep. The nurses hurried around, trying to change and feed as many babies as they could. The volunteer rockers remained in their chairs. It was the most beautiful and heartbreaking thing I'd ever seen.

Treyton

I lay in the dark hotel room staring up at the ceiling. I'd contemplated playing the piano in the lobby, but I knew sleep was near. I knew it would pull me under soon if I allowed it to.

My phone buzzed on my nightstand, the call lighting up my room. I reached over and checked the screen. I blinked hard at the sight of Brie's face on my phone. I'd taken a photo of her with her arms spread above her head in front of the Eiffel tower. I'd forgotten she'd made it her caller ID. The sight of her brought on a wave of sadness. As did the fact that she was calling me, and I knew I couldn't answer.

Brie's face disappeared from my screen and I lay in darkness once again.

That familiar emptiness I'd been feeling crept back into my chest. It had been weeks, and she hadn't called to apologize. Now, nothing she said could change my mind about what she'd done, even if I *had* found my voice as an advocate for children born to addicts.

My phone pinged. Brie had left a message.

Did I want to hear her voice? Did I want to hear what she had to say?

I opened the voicemail and played it.

"Treyton, it's Brielle. I'd be remiss if I didn't reach out to you."

My eyes narrowed at her formal tone.

"I've been contacted by the NICU coordinator at Las Vegas General. She asked me to come in to see their facility. I did and it's amazing, but it needs help. It would be a complete disservice if you decided not to make a donation to them because of me. This is about these babies. And these babies need you. The coordinator's name is Elaine and she's wonderful. I'm texting you her number. Please make the donation you told me you'd be willing to make. Do it for these babies."

The message ended, and I stared at my phone. Three weeks of silence and she reached out so I'd give money to a hospital. That was definitely the Brie I'd known for five years. No nonsense. Direct. Detached. I'd told her I didn't believe that's who she really was. But I was wrong. That's exactly who she was.

CHAPTER THIRTY

Treyton

"I'd like to make a toast," Z said as he raised his glass of beer at the head of the table.

The rest of the band, along with Aubrey, BJ, Arthur, and Reggie, lifted our glasses.

"To one hell of a world tour. Wouldn't have wanted to do it with anyone but this amazing group of people." His gaze circled the restaurant table, meeting each of our eyes, except Arthur, who we only tolerated.

"To the best lead singer a group could ever have," I called out.

"Coming from anyone else, I'd think that was sincere," Z shot back.

We all laughed and threw back our drinks.

This "last supper" was a tour ritual and always felt bittersweet. It was the end of our time together. We would now go our separate ways until we recorded our next album, had an appearance, or left for our next tour. Regardless which came first, I had a month off. And I had no fucking clue what I was going to do with so much time on my hands. Normally, I'd find some ladies to pass the time with. Now, I wasn't sure.

"Treyton?"

I glanced up.

Aubrey stared at me from across the table. "Have you talked to Brielle?" Her glassy eyes told me she'd had a lot to drink. She normally wouldn't ask me anything personal. That wasn't our relationship.

I shook my head. She hadn't asked if Brielle called. She asked if we'd *talked*, and we hadn't. "You?"

She shook her head, but I could see the sadness in her eyes.

And, as much as I appreciated Aubrey's loyalty to me, I felt bad that she'd lost her friend.

"Sucks what happened with her," Arthur slurred from beside me, his eyes glassier than Aubrey's.

"What?" I said.

"She quit the company."

"She quit the company?" Aubrey and I repeated at the same time.

He nodded. "It was time. Her father never wanted her to be part of his company to begin with."

Why the hell would she quit the company? The choice was the job or me. In the end, we ended up being a package deal, but that didn't mean she needed to quit the company. "Wasn't she going to take over once he retired?" I asked.

He balked. "God no. There's no way he'd let a woman take over the company he built from the ground up." Arthur threw back the rest of his drink. "Especially one he isn't even sure is his."

My mouth hung open. "What?"

"Oh, yeah. The talk in the office is he never believed Brielle was his. He was gone so much, he assumed his wife had cheated."

Holy. Shit. That would make sense. For a father to be such an asshole, there had to be more to it. I signaled for the waiter to bring Arthur another drink, suddenly wanting to keep him talking. "Does that mean he cheated on his wife when *he* was away?" I asked.

He scoffed. "Why do you think he lived in the city and not with his wife and Brielle?"

The waiter placed a new drink in front of Arthur who immediately took a long swallow.

"When Savage Beasts came along," he continued, his nose and cheeks now cherry red with the heat of the alcohol. "Brielle had just graduated from college and was begging for a job. He didn't want her working there, so we think he concocted a plan to watch her fail."

"What's that mean?" Aubrey asked.

"He assumed Savage Beasts would be a one-hit wonder," Arthur explained. "Then he could fire her for not doing a suitable job with their PR. He's a real son of a bitch like that."

Aubrey raised a brow at me, then turned to Arthur. "If she wanted to work there so badly, why do you think she quit the company? We were under the impression that when she left here, she started working with another band or something."

He shook his head. "When her father pulled that no fraternizing card then leaked Treyton's past to the press, she quit."

My eyes widened as a cold chill rushed up my spine. "Hold up. What'd you say?"

"She quit," he said.

"Before that," Aubrey and I said in unison.

"He leaked your past to the press," Arthur said, as if we should've known.

I fell back in my chair and dragged my hands through my hair. Her *father* leaked the information. I closed my eyes for a long moment, trying to control the sudden throbbing in my temples. She must've told him in a desperate attempt to change his mind about his ultimatum. But it didn't. It only gave the asshole ammo to hurt us both. "Fuck me."

Arthur looked between me and Aubrey. "What am I missing?"

With her face suddenly white as a ghost, Aubrey shook her head, realizing what we'd done. What we'd *all* done.

We fucked up.

Me worse than anyone.

CHAPTER THIRTY-ONE

Brielle

My phone rang, pulling me out of a deep sleep. Darkness filled my hotel room as my hand shot out from beneath the comforter. I grabbed the phone from my nightstand and squinted at the bright screen illuminating the room. My body stilled and my heartbeat accelerated at the sight of Trey's name on my phone.

What could he want?

He hadn't returned my call about the donation, nor had he called to apologize.

I wasn't in the mood to deal with him now, so I sent the call to voicemail and tossed my phone back on the nightstand.

Two minutes later my phone beeped, signifying a voice message.

Dammit.

It was one thing to not want to speak to him. It was something else entirely to know he'd left a message.

I reached for my phone, clicked on the voicemail, and put it on speaker.

"Brie…"

Trey's tortured voice sent a shiver coasting over me.

"I know you sent my call to voicemail and I don't even blame you…"

Damn right he couldn't blame me.

"I'm so damn sorry…"

I scoffed. *Now he's sorry?*

"You did nothing to deserve what I said…"

Agreed.

"I know it was your father."

You should've known that as soon as it happened.

"I screwed everything up."

I closed my eyes, a small sense of satisfaction sweeping over me. But I wouldn't allow myself to feel happiness over his regret. Over his delayed apology. He should have trusted me.

At least now the truth had come out.

"I want to see you. Face to face. I need you, Brie. I need you more than I realized." And just like that, the message ended.

I opened my eyes and lay there with my mind spinning. Did I believe him? Did I trust that he was truly sorry for doubting me? I wasn't someone who forgave easily. Trust was a difficult thing for me, and he had broken not only my trust but my heart too.

I needed him to regret hurting me. I needed him to feel the pain I'd felt after overhearing him and Z talk about me. I needed him to realize what he'd lost when he didn't trust me. And, I needed him to prove I was the only person in the world for him.

And maybe—just maybe—I'd be able to look him in the eyes and see the guy I once saw.

* * *

"You're still here?" a nurse who entered the family room in the NICU asked the following day.

"Still here," I said, scrolling the newsfeed on my phone as I ate a salad. I'd stayed in Las Vegas a week longer than I expected to, visiting Claire every day. I couldn't leave. I kept convincing myself she'd be okay, but then the next day I was right back there, holding her, feeding her, and comforting her.

My life was surely a mess.

I had no job.

No parents.

And, the closest person to me was a baby I'd soon be leaving.

Classic.

"Well, we love having you here," the nurse assured me as she grabbed a drink and walked out.

Knowing I was wanted there warmed a piece of my heart that had for a long time lay dormant. My last few weeks with the band, feeling like part of a family, had begun to awaken that feeling. But, that was short-lived, just like this would prove to be once I flew back home. To no job. And no one.

My finger stopped scrolling when a photo of Trey and a young man at a meet and greet in Monaco filled my screen. I skimmed the article beneath it. The young man was born to the same circumstance as Trey. Apparently, he and Trey had bonded.

At least something positive came from my father leaking his story. Now he could use his celebrity status for something good. Of course, he'd still mess around and get caught in compromising situations, but at least this would give him more of a purpose. He was a hell of a drummer, but that was superficial. What he'd use his abilities for—the greater purpose—was what truly mattered.

CHAPTER THIRTY-TWO

Brielle

I lay in the hotel bed my final night in Vegas watching Savage Beasts on the *Late Night Show*. It was their first U.S. appearance since returning from overseas—the last appearance I'd booked for them. I hadn't returned Trey's call. But, seeing him on television brought back a barrage of unresolved emotions. The host asked the guys about their next album, and Z fielded those questions.

"Treyton's been doing a lot of the writing lately," Z told the host.

"Oh, yeah?" The host looked to Trey beside Z on the sofa. "Treyton, what's motivated you to step up and help write?"

"A girl," Cam said from his stool behind the sofa.

The host smiled, and the studio audience broke into laughter. "A girl, huh? Anyone we know?"

Trey smiled and his eyes drifted to the camera for a brief moment. "No."

"So, what is it about her that has you inspired?" the host persisted.

"He screwed up and she won't take him back," Cam added.

My eyes widened as Trey's eyes cut to Cam, likely wanting to kick his ass.

"*Ohhhh*," the host said. "So, these are sad songs you're writing."

"They're not all sad," Trey said. "Some of them are hopeful."

The audience broke into a chorus of *Awwww*.

The host looked to the audience. "Did you all not hear? *He* screwed up."

The audience laughed.

"What'd you do?" the host asked Trey.

I sat up, my eyes locked on the screen. What would he say?

Trey shifted uncomfortably in his seat. "I didn't trust her when I should've." He looked into the camera again, purposely talking directly to me. "She's confident and strong and one of the most amazing people I've ever met. I blew it, but I'm not giving up."

The audience applauded his determination.

"Smart man," the host said. "When you find the right one, you gotta hold onto her."

The interview lasted a few more minutes. Then, the show cut to commercial.

I fell back onto the bed. Was he really not giving up?

* * *

Tears trickled down my cheeks as I rocked baby Claire for what I knew would be the last time.

I closed my eyes and hummed "Clair de Lune." Claire cooed, and my eyes opened. I smiled through the tears. Her eyes were opened, and she stared up at me. "Hi, pretty girl. Do you like my song?"

Her eyes didn't waver from mine. I would've given anything to know she'd be okay.

I continued humming as her eyes assessed my face. Was she memorizing me so she wouldn't forget me the way I'd been memorizing her?

Motion outside the nursery window caught my attention. I glanced up. A cold chill filled my body. Trey stood there. He didn't smile. He didn't wave. He just stared at the baby in my arms. My heartbeat thumped against the wall of my chest.

Elaine walked over to Trey, her face lighting up. Trey turned and spoke to her like he knew her, then the two of them disappeared.

My heartbeat thumped harder.

Claire fussed in my arms which meant she was hungry. I stood and walked on wobbly legs over to the formula counter, retrieving her bottle from the nurse.

I needed to pull it together.

I needed to keep my composure.

Babies like Claire needed Trey. They needed his donation. They needed the attention he could bring to this epidemic. And, regardless of how I felt about Trey, she needed him.

I sat back down and offered the bottle to Claire who eagerly took the formula. "You're one hungry girl, aren't you?" I said, watching her eyes drift close as she sucked it down. "Does it taste good?" I burped her a couple of times and offered up more formula.

"Gonna introduce me to your friend?"

I pulled in a silent breath before my eyes slowly lifted. I wanted to hate Trey, standing there all put together in his dark jeans and a button-down shirt. I wanted to tell him I hated him for what he'd done to me. But as he stood in the baby nursery, having flown to Vegas for no other reason than to clearly meet with Elaine after I'd asked him to, I couldn't. And it hurt me to admit that to myself. "This is Claire."

I saw the moment the name registered because his head flinched back.

"At least that's what I call her," I explained.

He tipped his head, gauging my expression carefully. "She didn't have a name?"

I shook my head. "Did you?"

He shook his head and something about knowing that tugged at my heart. Trey crouched in front of me and stared at Claire. "She's so tiny."

"She was two pounds when she was born." I checked the bottle and it was time to burp her. I pulled the bottle from her mouth, and her lips continued to suck. "Sorry, little lady," I said, adjusting her in my lap.

"Her mouth is still moving," Trey observed.

"Yeah. She does that." I rubbed her back in small circles.

"I thought you're supposed to hit them?"

"She doesn't need that." A small burp shot from her mouth. "See?" I turned her and offered her the bottle which she took right away.

Trey watched her suck away at the formula. "Elaine said you've been here every day."

I raked my teeth over my bottom lip, embarrassed to admit the truth. Would he think I was crazy? Would he think what happened overseas loosened a screw in my head? It didn't matter anymore. "Yup."

A long silence passed between us. A long *uncomfortable* silence.

"I'm sorry," Trey said.

My eyes flashed from Claire to him still crouched in front of me.

"I should have trusted you," he said, pain creasing the corners of his eyes.

Tears pricked my eyes, and I hated that they did. He'd hurt me. He'd turned his back on me. He couldn't just show up here after weeks of silence and expect my forgiveness. Life didn't work like that. *I* didn't work like that. "Not now, Trey."

He huffed his frustration. "When?"

"Don't ruin my time with Claire. I leave tonight."

He stood up and buried his hands in his pockets, looking down at us.

Was he going to turn his back on me again because he didn't get his way?

"Can I hold her?" he asked.

I closed my eyes, pained by his question. Pained by his apology. Pained by the sight of him in front of me. But something about him wanting to hold her made me stand up.

He took a step back.

"Where are you going?" I asked, sensing the sudden fear in his eyes. "Sit."

He took my place in the chair and held out his arms.

"Just relax your arms on your lap."

He did and I bent down and placed Claire into them. The smile that replaced the fear on Trey's face lightened the tightness clawing at my chest. Claire looked up at him and their gazes locked.

"Hi, little one," he said, seemingly mesmerized by the tiny baby in his arms. "I'm Brie's friend Trey…me and you have a lot in common…"

Tears welled in my eyes as I watched him talk to Claire, but I willed them back with every shred of strength I had left.

"I met my mom here," he continued. "She spent time rocking me the way Brie's been rocking you."

I turned away and pretended to look at something behind me so I could wipe away the rogue tear trailing down my cheek.

"My mom and Brie were very similar. She was kind like Brie. And funny. And, even though she was my mom, I can still say she was pretty, inside and out."

Claire cooed.

I spun around, not wanting to miss their interaction.

Trey stared down at her, smiling like I'd never seen him smile before.

I slipped out my phone and captured the moment. Trey was so lost in her eyes that he didn't even notice. I slipped my phone back into my pocket and watched Claire fall asleep in his arms.

He began to hum a song to her. I would've been lying if I said a tiny piece of my heart didn't thaw when it came to Trey. "You're a natural," I said.

He glanced up at me. "You think so?"

I nodded.

He stared at me for a long time, as if he was trying to say something with his gaze. "Go somewhere with me."

I closed my eyes. Didn't he understand I was angry at him? Didn't he understand I was sad to be leaving Claire? "I leave in a few hours."

"I didn't ask when you leave," he said. "I asked you to go somewhere with me."

"No"

"Stop being difficult."

"I'm not being difficult. I have a plane to catch."

He cocked his head. "There are plenty of flights out of Vegas. If you miss one, I can get you on the next one."

"I don't need *you* to get me on a flight."

"Look, I know I deserve all this hostility you're rocking right now, but I'm gonna ask you again. Brie, will you please go somewhere with me? There's something I want to show you."

I heaved a sigh, hating him so much in that moment. Why was he doing this now?

"I'll give you time to say goodbye to Claire," he said, standing and turning toward me with her.

I opened my arms to take her, but he didn't let her go.

"Goodbye, sweet little girl." He leaned down and pressed his lips to her forehead. "Your angel will swoop in just like mine did."

My stomach lurched, feeling like his words were a lie. Like I was letting her down. Who was going to take her? Who would want her?

Finally, he placed her into my arms. "I'll be outside."

I said nothing until he left the nursery. "Well, that was interesting, wasn't it?" I said to Claire. "Boys are nothing but trouble. I hope you don't have to learn that the hard way. I hope no one breaks your heart and you're surrounded by kindness always." My eyes welled up. "You are going to be very strong. What am I saying? You already are. What you've been through is worse than what most adults can endure. Don't let anything change that. Always be a fighter. Always know you deserve the best life has to offer." Tears streamed out of my eyes. "Look at Trey. He started out like you and look at him now. You can be and do anything you set your mind to." I leaned down and kissed her forehead, my tears dripping onto her face. "I will miss you, sweet Claire."

I walked her over to the nurse so she could place her back into her little bed. Claire's eyes remained closed as I passed her off, which made it easier. If she'd opened them, I would've taken it as her silent plea for me to stay, and I would've.

I stared down at her sleeping so soundly, knowing that's how I wanted to remember her. I turned away and wiped my tears, only to find Trey standing in the window. Most would've looked away to give me the privacy I needed, but not Trey. He watched me, his eyes never wavering from mine. I broke eye contact and walked to the door. Instead of going to him, I walked to Elaine's office.

She glanced up from her desk at me in the doorway. "You okay?"

I nodded. "You'll let me know if anyone adopts her?"

She tilted her head in a motherly way which almost brought on more tears. "Of course."

I nodded, wiping away at my tears. "Thank you for everything, Elaine." I grabbed the handle on my carry-on luggage I'd stored in her office.

"It's me who should be thanking you," she said. "Your friend's an angel."

CHAPTER THIRTY-THREE

Brielle

Trey stood down the hallway, his hands buried in the pockets of his jeans.

I walked toward him, pulling my luggage behind me. I didn't even bother wiping the tear stains from my cheeks. What was the point? He'd seen my sadness. Hell, he was partially to blame for my sadness. I stopped in front of him, tipping back my head to meet his gaze. "What did you do?"

He stepped forward to hug me.

I stepped back, needing to stand my ground.

He lowered his arms, and I couldn't miss the hurt emanating from his eyes. He grabbed my carry-on. "I have a car downstairs. We'll talk in there," he said before walking toward the elevator with my luggage.

I followed behind, each step away from the nursery more difficult than the last. The elevator dinged once we reached it. Trey grabbed hold of my hand and walked us inside. I tried to release my hand from his, but he held on tighter. I wondered if he thought the strength of his grasp would give me the strength to leave.

Inside the elevator, neither of us spoke. I knew where my thoughts were, but where were his? I wanted him to release my hand now that we'd left the NICU, but he didn't. Even after we stepped into the lobby, he led me to the exit with my hand in his.

He finally released my hand as we stepped outside into the late afternoon sunlight. I squinted as he grabbed hold of the passenger door handle on a fancy sports car parked at the curb and pulled open the door for me. I stared inside the car, wondering if I was making the right decision by going somewhere with him.

I couldn't stand there deliberating all day so I did the only thing I could. I climbed inside.

Trey closed my door, placed my belongings in the trunk, then slid into the driver's seat. He turned to me, a hundred emotions racing across his face, but he said nothing. He switched on the engine, and the car purred to life. He pulled out into city traffic. I expected him to drive toward the Vegas lights, but he drove nowhere near them, opting for endless desert roads.

Nothing but the low purr of the expensive sports car filled the space around us. I said nothing, just gazed out the window as the desolate Nevada scenery blurred by. The sun lowered in the distance leaving an orange glow over the horizon.

"What went down with your dad?" Trey asked, breaking the silence.

"What do you mean?"

"I heard you quit his company."

"*And* being his daughter."

"Yeah?"

"I wanted nothing to do with him after what he did to you." I finally turned to Trey, knowing what I needed to say. "I'm sorry I told him about your past. At the time, I thought it would help him see you as more of a person and not just a pawn in his ultimatum."

"You couldn't have known he'd run to the press," he said. "I'm just sorry you lost your dad in the process."

I shrugged. "He was never a real dad. A real dad snuggles with his kid. A real dad paints with his kid even if he hates painting. A real dad puts on a tutu because it will make his kid laugh. Mine never did any of that."

"I'm sorry."

I shrugged. "You can't miss something you never had."

"Do you miss *us*?"

I looked back out the window. And, after a long pause, I nodded.

Trey reached over and took my hand. "Then take another chance on me, Brie."

After everything that went down, could it be that easy?

Trey switched on his blinker and turned into a neighborhood filled with small identical houses. He pulled over in front of a beige house with green shutters.

I stared out at the house, wondering where he'd taken me. My eyes moved over the small house with its tiny yard filled with rocks.

"My mom brought me back here to the first house I lived in," he explained. "She told me about the room upstairs where she rocked and sang to me after adopting me and bringing me home from the hospital. She told me this neighborhood wasn't right for me. That this house wasn't right for me. She said I needed someplace that I could run in a grass backyard and fit a piano in the sitting room. I don't think they could even afford to move to Tennessee, but they up and moved so *I'd* have a better life."

My eyes cut to his, not knowing what he wanted me to say.

"Life takes crazy turns, Brie. It deals us curveballs, and it places people in our lives who we never expected to meet."

My eyes stayed on his, letting him finish his thought.

"I never planned on you, Brie. But I'm so damn happy you worked your way into my heart. You challenged me and pissed me off and made me feel something for someone other than myself."

Tears pricked my eyes, but I forced them back with every bit of strength I had.

"You've got to know I didn't mean to hurt you. I just felt…blindsided. It was like the one person I was letting in had turned on me and taken advantage of me opening up."

"That's not me," I said.

He nodded. "I get that now."

"You should've gotten that before."

"I know." His tone matched his pained expression. "It kills me that I let you walk out of my life. Because when you left, you took a chunk of my heart I didn't even know I'd miss. Since my parents died, I've needed no one but Z. I didn't want to need you. But I did. I *do*." He released my hand and reached in the back seat, grabbing a manila envelope and handing it to me.

"What is it?"

"Something I should've done sooner."

I unfastened the seal on the envelope and reached inside, pulling out a thick packet of stapled papers. I read the words on the cover sheet and my eyes widened. I was looking at a contract opt-out.

"I wanted to be the one to tell you," he said.

My eyes snapped to his.

"We didn't have a termination clause in our contract. We're done with Artists Limited."

"But…"

"We're in the market for a new publicist. And, we want *you*, if you accept our offer." He lifted his chin toward the papers in my hand. "It's in there."

I flipped through the packet, finding the contract they'd written up and the salary they were offering. It was double what I'd been making. "You can't be serious?"

"Which part?"

I shook my head, not knowing what to say.

"Is that a no?"

A mixture of sadness and hope bubbled inside of me as I turned to him. "What happens next time? What happens in a month from now when someone says I said something? Will you take their word or mine?"

"What do you want to hear?"

"What do I *really* want to hear?"

He nodded.

"I really want to hear that you're helping the hospital. That you know how important it is to draw awareness to the epidemic that plagued you as a child."

"Done."

"What?"

"The band already made a million-dollar donation to the hospital."

My eyes widened.

"And I'm working with Elaine to start a foundation to aid babies born like me and Claire, as well as the adoptive parents who are conflicted about adopting them. We're going to ensure they receive continued support throughout the life of these children. They won't just be handed over without the proper services in place to help both the children and their adoptive parents."

Tears stung my eyes.

"That's the biggest problem," he continued. "These adoptive parents are left unequipped to deal with the effects of drug addiction. They'll get whatever they need now. Our foundation will make sure of it."

Tears leaked out of my eyes, flowing freely now.

Trey reached up and tried to wipe them away, but they kept falling. "Stop crying, Brie. You're scaring me."

"Why?" I asked.

"Because big bad Brie does not cry."

I laughed through my tears. "They're happy tears."

His brows shot up. "Does that mean I'm forgiven?"

I shook my head.

He cupped my cheeks and dropped his forehead to mine. "Cut the shit, Brie. You're mine. No matter how difficult you're being right now, you know it's happening. Me and you."

"You broke my heart."

"And I'll *never* do it again."

"I don't believe you."

He pulled his forehead back so he could look me in the eyes. "Dammit, Brie. I was pissed at you for taking the rapper's side over mine, but I got over it. I got over it because I knew deep down I had feelings for you that I couldn't fight any longer. Don't you still have feelings for me? Don't you think I deserve forgiveness too?"

My chest heaved as everything he'd said rushed at me at once.

"You're going to have to learn to trust me, Brie."

He wasn't wrong. I was being a complete hypocrite. "You're right."

"Say that again."

"You're right. I never should've doubted *you*."

His brows shot up.

"So, I guess that means we're even," I said.

A smile slipped across his face. "You gonna be my girl again, Brie?"

I stared into his hopeful eyes, knowing I couldn't stay away from him any longer. He wanted one thing in this world, and it was a family. I had a sudden urge to be part of that family. "I—"

He didn't let me finish. His mouth crashed down on mine. His lips and tongue, mixed with the salt from my tears, made for the perfect kiss. One that carried so many emotions. Regret. Forgiveness. And love. A whole lot of love.

CHAPTER THIRTY-FOUR

Six Months Later

Brielle

I sat on a leather sofa in the recording studio listening to Trey lay down piano tracks for their next album. Trey had been so brave to suggest it, knowing pianos and rock bands didn't necessarily go together. But the guys loved the idea. None of them but Z had even known how talented Trey really was.

And just like Guns and Roses had done with "November Rain," Trey sat behind the piano adding a beautiful instrumental to the beginning of their soon-to-be-hit-song, "Apologies."

He finished and glanced to me on the other side of the glass behind the producers sitting at the soundboards. "What'd you think?"

"Good," one of the producers said.

"I was talking to my girl," Trey informed him.

I smiled. It had been six months and still those butterflies swarmed in my belly when he called me his girl—*or* showed that he cared more about what I thought than anyone else. "It sounded amazing."

"Obviously," he said, cocky as ever.

I laughed and shook my head as he began playing another piece.

I sat back, letting the beautiful sound drift over me as I reflected on the last six months and how much more in love with Trey I grew each day. I understood what Aubrey meant now when she said her and Z hadn't started that way. It came with time. With knowing all the little things no one else knew.

My phone buzzed with an incoming call. I opened my eyes and grabbed it from the sofa beside me. *Elaine.* I gasped, quickly accepting the call. "Hi, Elaine. Is Claire okay?"

"That's the reason for my call."

My heart began to race.

"She's being discharged."

The hair on the back of my neck stood on end. "To child services?"

"No. We have parents lined up for adoption."

"What?" Elation mixed with sadness swept over me. She'd have parents but belong to someone else.

"The adoptive parents are going to be finalizing the paperwork this week and then taking her home."

Tears pricked my eyes, unprepared for the news. "I thought adoption is a long process?"

"Not in these cases. She's a custody of the state. If there are parents willing to have her and their background, references, and other credentials can be expedited and if it all comes out clean, they can have her whenever she's healthy enough to go to her new home."

"Can I see her first?"

"That's why I'm calling. I wasn't sure if you'd be able to get here."

"I'm coming now." I disconnected the call and checked for flights.

Tapping on the glass caught my attention. I glanced up from my phone. Trey stood with questioning eyes. I motioned him out and he quickly stepped out of the recording studio. "What's wrong?"

"Claire's been adopted."

He held out his hand to me. "Let's go."

* * *

We hurried through the hospital to the NICU. Too many emotions rushed through me. I knew I'd said goodbye to Claire before leaving Las Vegas—every time I'd visited over the last six months. Yes, I'd been back. Flights were cheap, and I had no reason *not* to check on her. But now I'd be saying goodbye forever. She'd move wherever her adoptive parents lived and not even remember me.

In the back of my mind, I always thought she'd be there, and I could fly to Vegas to see her. Now I realized that would never happen again.

Trey and I made our way toward the nursery window. I stopped short, peering in at the babies, searching for Claire while Trey went to find Elaine. My eyes frantically looked from baby to baby, but I couldn't find her.

"Brielle?" Elaine said.

I twisted away from the window.

"You okay?" she asked moving toward me.

I nodded. "I'm so happy she'll have a good home— she *will* have a good home, won't she?"

She smiled. "I've been assured of it."

I released a breath. "Her adoptive parents are going to fall in love with her."

"They already have," she assured me. "Why don't you go in and hold her. She's in the family room."

I moved away from Elaine and made my way into the family room, stopping once I stumbled upon an unexpected sight. Trey sat rocking Claire.

Trey looked up when he heard me approach. "She's sleeping," he whispered.

"Elaine said she'll be going to a good home," I told him, as I walked over to them.

He nodded. "I'm sure she will."

"May I?" I asked, holding out my arms to take her.

He shook his head. "I need to talk to you first." He stood and placed her into the bassinet. Then, he turned to me and grabbed my hands. "You know as well as I do that Claire was put into our lives for a reason."

"What?"

"Something happened when I saw her in your arms that first time," he said. "It was like…it was supposed to be that way."

I stilled, my heartbeat accelerating. "What are you saying?"

"Then I held her and understood what happened when my mom looked at me." He tipped his head to the side and stared into my eyes like I should've understood. "I've been in contact with Elaine every week."

"What?"

"I wanna wear a tutu to make Claire smile."

My brows shot up.

"I want to paint with her and mess up our clothes," he continued. "And I want to snuggle with her so she'll know how loved she is."

My breath caught in my throat.

"She's ours, Brie," he said. "It hasn't been easy, but they finally approved all my paperwork. I even had an interview."

No. No. Nooooo.

"Claire is *ours*," he repeated.

I shook my head, my mind spinning with the crazy words leaving his mouth. "You're a rock star. You can't care for a baby. You can't even take care of yourself half the time."

He cocked his head, unamused by my dig.

"You're away more than you're home."

"That doesn't have to be the case. The band has no reason to tour the way we've been touring."

"Of course you do. It's your job," I said.

"Tell me you haven't thought about it, Brie. Tell me you haven't thought about having Claire for real."

"I mean…I'm obviously drawn to her, but—"

"Can't you see this all happened for a reason? It's how it's supposed to be. Me, you, and Claire."

Suddenly, the room felt too small. Too suffocating. Too everything.

I spun away from Trey and bolted out of the room and down the hallway, needing to catch my breath. Was he *insane*? Had he lost his *mind*? Was he *on* something? This was nuts!

The padding of Trey's feet followed after me. "Brie."

I kept walking, needing to be away from this lunatic disguised as a rock star.

"God dammit, Brie. *Stop.*"

I quickened my pace. He had no idea what he was even saying.

He grabbed hold of my arm, tugging me back to him. "What are you doing?"

"Getting away from you."

"Why?"

"Because you're scaring me."

His forehead creased. "Scaring you?"

"You can't make promises like that."

"Why not?"

I tipped my head, the obviousness of his question not requiring words. He was giving me hope. Hope I had no business having. Hope I didn't even realize I wanted. He was making me see a life I had no business seeing.

Damn him.

"I don't know how to care for a baby," I said.

"I've seen you with Claire. You're amazing."

"I can feed and burp her. It takes more than that to raise a child."

"Then we'll learn…" he assured me. "Together."

I had no idea what to say. No idea what I was even thinking.

"Give me one good reason why we shouldn't do this?" he said.

"How about we're not married?"

His lips slipped into a smirk, and he slowly lowered himself down onto one knee.

I gasped.

He pulled a ring out of his pocket and held it up. "Marry me, Brie. Be my family and I'll be yours."

My right palm flew to my mouth.

"I love you," he said, taking my left hand. "Can't you see this will be our greatest adventure yet?" The sincerity in his words and this grand gesture rendered me speechless. "Just say yes, Brie."

My heart raced and tears trailed down my cheeks. Was this really happening? I stared down into his beautiful blue eyes seeing a real future with this man…and Claire. It didn't have to be crazy. I closed my eyes and did the only thing I could do in that moment. I nodded.

He slipped the ring onto my finger and stood up, wrapping me in his arms before I could even look at the monstrosity he'd given me.

"You're crazy," I said.

"You're marrying me. What does that make you?"

"Too far gone to say no."

He pulled back and gazed down at me with his cocky smirk firmly in place. Then, slowly, he leaned down and our lips touched.

I melted into his kiss—my *fiancé's* kiss.

I knew with complete certainty that my life as I knew it would never be the same.

EPILOGUE

One Year Later

Brielle

The bass from Trey's drums pounded through my body as I stood backstage watching Savage Beasts perform in New York City. Claire lay asleep in my arms with noise-cancelling headphones on her ears. It amazed me how she could sleep through her dad's shows, but night after night she did.

Claire was an easy baby, which made me worry she'd be a difficult toddler. But so far so good. The doctors assured us she was hitting every milestone. That knowledge elated us.

The crowd's applause erupted, and I strained my neck to see what was happening on stage.

Trey slipped behind the piano they added to the stage for this tour. He began the intro to "What Happens in a Dive Bar," their final encore song. Night after night I watched the fans sway to the piano instrumental of the song inspired by our first night together.

Once the final note of his instrumental floated through the arena, Trey jumped up from the piano and took his seat behind the drums, smacking his drumsticks together so the band could join in on the song.

The guys brought down the house, rocking New York like never before. They finished their encore, said their good nights to the deafening applause and cheers from their fans, and made their way backstage.

Z passed me first, stopping to drop a kiss on the top of Claire's head. "It amazes me that she doesn't want to watch her godfather kill it night after night."

"And it amazes me that her godfather can fit through the door with such an enormous head," I countered.

Z laughed. "You love me."

I rolled my eyes. "Sometimes."

Cam passed me next, dropping an unexpected kiss on my cheek.

I spun around. "Watch it, Cam, or my husband will kick your ass."

"You think I'm scared of him? The guy's turned into a mega-wuss since he married you." He backed right into Trey.

"Wuss?" Trey asked, before shoving him away and walking over to me and Claire. He dropped a kiss on my lips before placing a soft kiss on the top of Claire's blonde head. "How'd my girls enjoy the show?"

"It was great," I said. "But don't forget the PSA you're filming once the fans clear out."

"I love it when your mom gives me orders," he whispered to Claire. "Especially in the bedroom." His brows bounced as he looked to me.

I rolled my eyes.

"Treyton," a voice called.

Trey and I turned to find Matteo—his fan from Monaco—and his dad walking our way. Matteo was decked out in Savage Beasts wear that Trey sent him every time something new came out.

"Hey, Buddy." Trey smiled. "What'd you think of the show?"

Matteo began to lift his thumb, but when Trey cocked his head, he stopped and flashed a toothy grin. "Awe…some."

Trey lifted his hand and Matteo slapped it. Trey was so proud of Matteo's progress, and thanks to the foundation he'd started, kids like Matteo were getting free treatments and counseling. "You ready to film this PSA with me and my daughter?"

Matteo began to lift his thumb but stopped. "Ye…sssss."

"You better remember me once you get famous," Trey teased him.

Matteo snorted and clapped his hands.

The film crew emerged by the stage, and the director approached me, making sure we were good to go. I handed Claire off to Trey who removed her headphones and walked out onto the stage with Matteo, his dad, and the director. The crew moved some chairs to the front of the stage to showcase the set. The director motioned Trey over, pointing to the chair on the right. Trey sat with Claire asleep in his arms. The director motioned Matteo into the seat beside Trey.

"Just act natural," the director told them as he moved behind the monitor beside the camera. "Ready?"

Trey and Matteo nodded.

"Action," the director called.

Trey looked right into the camera and said, "Don't let your past define you."

As he spoke the dialogue he'd rehearsed for days leading up to the filming, I couldn't harness the pride that came from watching him give a voice to the epidemic that had afflicted him as a child. He'd done so much good since the revelation of his past. Kids like Matteo had begun to get the treatment their adoptive parents didn't even know existed—or they didn't have the means to secure. With Trey's foundation, these parents and kids had a sense of hope they hadn't had before.

"Cut," the director called once Trey finished his message.

Trey's eyes immediately sought mine.

I nodded my approval, my face beaming with pride.

Claire chose that moment to wake up. Trey lifted her in front of him so she looked him in the eyes. Her soft giggle floated to where I stood and my heart swelled. I never knew I was capable of feeling such love for two human beings. But Trey and Claire had stolen my heart.

Trey stood and approached me. "Where were you just now?"

"What?"

"You were thinking about something."

I rolled my eyes, hating how good he was at reading me.

"Tell me," he urged.

"First of all, you did an amazing job out there."

"Brie. This is me. Of course I was amazing."

I growled. "If I didn't love you so much, I'd hate you."

He chuckled. "I'm waiting."

"Fine. I was just thinking about you and Claire. And how you've stolen my heart."

He stared back at me, his eyes narrowed on mine.

"What are *you* thinking?" I asked.

"I'm not giving it back."

My nose scrunched. "What?"

"Your heart. If I've stolen it, I'm not giving it back. It's mine and I'm keeping it forever."

I tilted my head. The vulnerability emanating from my husband's eyes nearly brought me to my knees. "Good. Because I don't want it back."

He smiled, the vulnerability disappearing as he leaned in and pressed his lips to mine. "I love you, Brie Collins."

"I know."

Claire giggled and we pulled apart, staring at her cute little face.

We had the same idea, both leaning in and kissing her on opposite cheeks. She giggled again.

I pulled in a deep cleansing breath, letting it fill me with all the happiness these two brought into my life.

They were my family.

The only family I'd ever need.

THE END

OTHER TITLES BY J. NATHAN

If you enjoyed Treyton and Brielle's story,
check out Aubrey and Kozart's story,
Kozart (Book #1 in the Savage Beasts standalone series)

For You standalone series:
Book #1 *For Finlay*
Book #2 *For Forester*
Book #3 *For Crosby*
Book #4 *For Emery*

Standalones
Seren
Something About You
I Just Need You
You're the Reason
Until Alex
Since Drew
Before Hadley

ACKNOWLEDGEMENTS

Thank you so much for taking the time to read Treyton and Brielle's story. I always try to give you a story I would want to read, so I hope you enjoyed it!

To all the bloggers and readers who continue to share my books. Thank you a hundred times over! I could not do this without you!

To my wonderful ARC team members who anxiously await each new novel I write. Thank you for giving me the inspiration to give you the best that I've got. And thank you for taking the time to read, review, and spread the word. It means the world to me!

To my always wonderful beta readers: Dali, Renee, Mimi Jean, Kim, Kerrie, and Heather. Thank you for reading *Treyton* when it wasn't the polished story it is now!! I know I can count on you to give it to me straight.

To my editor Stephanie Elliot. Thank you for your honesty. I love reading your reactions to something you like, but even more so to something you don't like. You make my work better! I'm so lucky to have you in my life!

To Gemma at Gem's Precise Proofreads. Thank you for your great eye for detail! You are a true pro at what you do, and I am so happy to have found you! Thanks for loving Trey as much as you love Kozart. That is *definitely* saying something!

To my wonderful PA Renee. You keep me organized and always give me the truth whether I want to hear it or not. You also make me laugh every day! Thank you for being in my life!

To Peggy with your keen eye for detail. Thank you for catching those last few mistakes!! I am so lucky to have you on my team!

To Tiffany at T.E. Black Designs for creating another beautiful cover and Eric McKinney for the gorgeous cover photo.

And last, but never least, to my family. Thank you for always loving and supporting me. I know how truly lucky I am to have all of you!

ABOUT THE AUTHOR

J. Nathan resides on the east coast with her husband and soon to be ten-year-old son. She is an avid reader of all things romance. Happy endings are a must. Alpha males with chips on their shoulders are an added bonus. When she's not curled up with a good book, she can be found spending time with family and friends, at soccer and baseball games, and working on her next novel.